ST. MARTIN'S

MINOTAUR

MYSTERIES

THE IRISH CAIRN MURDER

"Shows off some intricate plotting and a cast of eccentrics, including Jasper, Tunet's overweight gourmand boyfriend, and her rival, the inept and vengeful Inspector O'Hare."

—*Publishers Weekly*

THE IRISH MANOR HOUSE MURDER

"Good writing, all the twists and turns of a complicated plot, peopled with well-rounded characters . . . should satisfy the most discriminating mystery lover."

—*The Tampa Tribune*

"Interesting characters keep one moving through the labyrinthine plot, and the local color is the green and silvered gray of Ireland."

—*Booklist*

THE IRISH COTTAGE MURDER

"There are easily enough plots, subplots, and full-bodied characters to supply a half-dozen novels. An excess of riches, then, in a most promising debut."

—*Kirkus Reviews*

"Every page has a new discovery, a surprise, a twist, a new character revelation. And the solution to the mystery is as convincing as it is unexpected."

—*Pittsburgh Post-Gazette*

Be Sure to Read These Riveting
Torrey Tunet Mysteries
by Dicey Deere

The Irish Manor House Murder

The Irish Cottage Murder

Available From
St. Martin's/Minotaur Paperbacks

The
Irish Cairn
Murder

Dicey Deere

St. Martin's Paperbacks

THE IRISH CAIRN MURDER

Library of Congress Catalog Card Number: 2001057712

ISBN: 0-312-98316-6

Printed in the United States of America

St. Martin's Press hardcover edition / May 2002
St. Martin's Paperbacks edition / March 2003

St. Martin's Paperbacks are published by St. Martin's Press, 175 Fifth
Avenue, New York, NY 10010.

10 9 8 7 6 5 4 3 2 1

To Bruce and Florence
and to Jennifer and Miles
and to Chester-from-Dublin

1

From where he stood hidden among the trees, he could see the cottage. The American girl was leaning against the door-post in the sunlight. She wore a red turtle-necked sweater and jeans. She was chatting with her worker, the boy, as he cut lengths of lumber on a plank set up on two sawhorses. Ah, the boy! Dakin. Tall for a sixteen-year-old. Dark-haired, narrowly built. The photos had shown an aristocratic-looking face with a high-bridged nose. Aristocratic. A bit of irony there.

A few feet from Dakin, a kid in skinny black pants and sweatshirt and wearing a brimmed cap was sitting on a log, whittling. It would be Dakin's sister, maybe ten years old. She didn't concern him. It was Dakin. Only him. Dakin was the key. So easy! So easy!

He pinched out his cigarette, unfolded his cell phone, and dialed. Watching, he saw the American girl an instant later lift her head at the sound of the ringing phone. She said a word to Dakin, then turned and went into the cottage.

Torrey came from the cottage and held out her portable phone. "Dakin? It's for you." She smiled at him. There was a faint blue bruise on his cheekbone, courtesy of the bigger of the two young thugs who'd yesterday tried to knock her off

1

her new Peugeot bike on the access road. Pedaling on the road with her groceries from Ballynagh, she'd seen the driver of the Dublin-to-Cork bus order the pair of them off the bus, heard his furious "Off my bus with yor fookin' drugs!" Then, standing on the road, they'd spotted her. Well, too bad for them—and lucky for her—that two minutes later Dakin, then a stranger to her, had happened along on foot.

Funny, the coincidence, that it was Dakin who'd turned up this afternoon. Last night she'd called Winifred Moore up at Castle Moore. It was mid-October and unexpectedly cold. She'd built a fire of peat and coal to warm the kitchen, but a kitchen window frame, well over a hundred years old, and rotting, had collapsed, letting in drafts of icy air. She'd needed a carpenter. In the village, a half mile down the road, smoke rose from chimneys up and down Butler Street, from O'Malley's Pub to Miss Amelia's Tea Shoppe, to Nolan's Bed and Breakfast.

"Lucky you called me," Winifred had said. "I've somebody who does carpentry. He's just finishing up a bit of work for me; I'll send him over tomorrow afternoon."

Dakin had arrived at three o'clock next day, his kid sister tagging along. *"You!"* Torrey had said, and laughed with pleasure at seeing her defender again, but sorry about the blue bruise on his cheekbone in her defense. The Peugeot had been new, she'd paid three hundred pounds for it. But it was the ugliness of the encounter, something feral in the two boys on pipestem legs and in leather jackets who'd wanted the bike—or her?—that had been so disturbing. Anyway, it was over. Yesterday's news.

By four o'clock, when the phone call came for Dakin, he had measured and cut narrow lengths of lumber for a new window frame, carefully selecting pieces from a miscellany in the back of his jeep. The sun shone down on his dark head. Torrey, handing him the phone, was thinking of offering him

2

and his little sister a mug of hot cider, maybe with a cinnamon stick; she was sure she had a jar of —

"If *what*?" Dakin, holding the phone to his ear, listening, was staring blankly back at Torrey, his eyes wide, startled, "If I don't *what*? You'll *what*? My mother? Are you crazy? Who is this? I said, *who*—" He broke off. Torrey could hear the crackle of the caller's voice. Abruptly Dakin clicked off the phone.

At once the phone rang again. Torrey looked questioningly at Dakin. His face had gone pale, perspiration dampened his brow, he looked sick. Something cruel and ugly was happening. The phone kept ringing. "Shall I? . . ." Torrey began, and hesitated, looking at Dakin. He shook his head.

But because Torrey was who she was, she impulsively snatched the phone from him, clicked it on, and said sharply into the receiver, "Enough of that! Who is this?"

Silence. Then, "Ah," the voice said softly, a man's voice, "you who live in that groundsman's cottage. Meddling, are you? Unwise. Even dangerous." A monotone, the voice, it made her shiver. She knew the accent. Couldn't quite place it.

"You—" she began. But the phone went dead.

A half hour later, at four-thirty, the lengths of wood mitered and stacked just inside the cottage door, Dakin left, trailed by Lucinda, his kid sister. Tomorrow he'd build the frame. Torrey had learned nothing about the phone call. "What is it?" she'd asked him. "Anything I can do?" But he'd only managed a stiff, "No, thanks."

"Well, then, tomorrow. Four o'clock. Right?"

"Yes." Automatic as a robot. His hazel eyes, under dark brows, were troubled. His mind was somewhere else. His mustard-colored jersey was wet with sweat. He shrugged into his jacket.

Torrey waited until Dakin and his sister were out of sight.

3

Then she walked west toward where the woods were thickest. When she'd picked up the ringing phone in the cottage, she'd been facing the window and had glanced out. Something had glinted from the woods. Maybe the dying sun reflecting on a glass bottle someone had thrown away. Still—

She stood now beside a leafy oak a hundred yards from the cottage. Nothing here. Only bent grass that might have been where a rabbit had lain, or a chipmunk.

But neither a rabbit nor a chipmunk smoked cigarettes. She bent down and looked closer. A cigarette butt. She picked it up. Too dark now, under the oak, to read the brand. She wrapped the cigarette butt in a crumpled tissue from her jeans pocket.

She stood a moment then, looking about. Leaves rustled, twigs snapped, an unidentified animal squealed. What was she doing out here in the woods, the frosty evening drawing in, so that she shivered? It was none of her business. But the boy's appalled face! Dakin Cameron, her rescuer, her worker, whom she liked so much. Who was he?

Back at the cottage, Torrey turned on lights and drew the kitchen curtains closed. Then irresolute, she stood. She ought to call Inspector O'Hare at the Ballynagh police station.

But . . . to report what? To report a phone call that she suspected Dakin Cameron would deny had been threatening? Or . . . how do you report an apprehension?

Besides, Inspector O'Hare didn't view her fondly. She'd seen him raise his eyes to heaven at sight of her. They were enemy beasts who'd met in a forest, she and O'Hare. She was a professional interpreter. A year ago, she'd bested him, solving a murder with her knowledge of foreign languages. Even more exasperating to Inspector O'Hare was that he knew of her past as a thief. It was no wonder he wished she'd disappear in a puff of smoke.

"Well, too bad, my dear Inspector," Torrey said aloud, "Because here I'm staying." She'd fallen in love with the cottage two years ago. She had been on an interpreting job in Dublin, neutral ground for a Mideast conference, when she'd first seen the decrepit old groundsman's cottage with its latticed windows. The cottage was a ten-minute bike ride from the village of Ballynagh in this northwest corner of Wicklow. Now it was her jumping-off place for her interpreting assignments in Europe. Someday she'd return to the States. But not now. Not yet.

Seven o'clock, already full dark. Outside, a wind had sprung up; a cold draft came in through the damaged window. Torrey rolled up an old sweater and stuffed it around the window frame. She started a fire in the fireplace next to the bake oven, adding coal to the peat to make the fire last longer. She'd arrived back at the cottage only two days ago from an interpreting assignment in Prague. Besides the bedroom and tiny bath, there was just the kitchen with its worn old couch and chairs.

It had smelled damp and unlived-in. In the bedroom, the cotton rug looked as though gnawed by mice. Arriving late, she'd dined at the kitchen table on a can of sardines and some soda crackers she'd had in a tin, and a pot of tea. She'd felt comfortably relaxed. Two weeks before her next assignment. Budapest. She'd have to bone up a bit on her Hungarian. So in Dublin, on the way to Ballynagh, she'd stopped at Waterstone's Bookshop on Nassau Street and bought three Georges Simenon *Inspector Maigret* paperbacks that had been translated into Hungarian. Before each interpreting assignment, she liked to read a Simenon or two in that particular language to reinforce her facility in it. Luckily, Simenon had been published in fifty languages. Not that she herself knew more than a handful of languages. So far. Though she'd stud-

5

ied hard for years. A linguistics professor at Harvard had written a paper about her, explaining that her facility with languages was genetic. Was it? She had no idea. But Interpreters International in Boston kept the assignments coming, *mirabile dictu*. Wonderful to relate.

Before going to bed, she'd unpacked the jump rope from her luggage. It weighed four ounces, and she was never without it. Sometimes, skipping rope was sheer enjoyment, and it kept her fit. She was twenty-seven, sleek and slim, despite being hooked on chocolate bars with almonds and on pasta with gorgonzola. She kept her dark wavy hair short; it was easier to handle when she traveled on assignments. Her eyes were gray, and her eyelashes, though short, were so black that they starred her eyes, a startling effect, so she didn't have to bother with mascara.

Other times, skipping rope seemed to help her think. And often it made her remember her happy childhood in North Hawk, happy only until the day when she was eleven and her Romanian father departed the town, deserting her and her seamstress mother who'd borne the New England name of Hapgood. Vlad Tunet, watchmaker. *Tunet*, "thunder" in Romanian. An adventurer, looking for fortune, to whom Torrey's mother had been that beloved fortune for twelve years, until his restlessness won. Skipping rope, Torrey could often see him laughing, the white teeth a brilliant slash in his tanned face. He'd kissed the top of her head before he left, and given her the scarf. The peacock bandana, as she thought of it. Silk. Turquoise-and-gold peacocks, outlined in black and splashed with silver streaks. Through the years she wore it often; sometimes around her waist, sometimes as a scarf, most often as a bandana. Strange that the peacock scarf gave her a sense of security when her father had deserted her and her mother to go off adventuring. Was his search for adventure something in his blood? And hers? As for her poor dear mother, surprisingly, instead of pining for Vlad Tunet, she had married the North Hawk pharmacist.

Torrey, yawning, had hung the jump rope and the peacock scarf on the pegs beside the kitchen door and gone early to bed.

She'd slept well. The next day had dawned brisk and sunny. She'd pedaled off to Ballynagh on the Peugeot for groceries; on the way back, she'd been stopped by the two trouble-seeking lads who'd been thrown off the bus. Thank God for Dakin!

Now, standing beside the kitchen table, Torrey took the tissue from her jeans pocket and unwrapped the cigarette butt. It was a brand she didn't recognize. Sinbad. She put it in a cup on the dresser.

In the fireplace, a bar of peat shifted with a soft, whispering sound. The kitchen had warmed up. Suppertime.

Corn soup. Out of a can. What about putting pepper in it? Or curry? Jasper would know.

Jasper. "My Irish lover," Torrey said aloud, smiling. Jasper, a dozen pounds overweight, with navy blue eyes and dark curly hair that was already receding though he was only thirty-six. Jasper, who handled two jobs that never acknowledged each other: He was Jasper who wrote a weekly culinary column in the *Irish Independent*. He was also Jasper Shaw, the investigative reporter.

Curry. Or maybe dill? Where *was* Jasper?

She put down the can of soup. At her desk in the corner she tapped into her E-mail. Well, well! A message from Jasper:

My darling, my love, try this: Boil leeks twelve minutes, drizzle with melted butter mixed with a teaspoonful of Dijon mustard. Sprinkle of Parmesan. Am in Belfast, the usual political contretemps. Arriving in Ballynagh next week with my winning ways . . . you to be wooed and won again.

7

"That's *wooed*," Torrey said aloud. "Wooed!"

At ten o'clock she went to bed. Half-asleep she thought, *Dakin Cameron*. She saw the alarm in his eyes, saw his face go pale. Yes, first thing tomorrow. Winifred, at Castle Moore.

2

"Who's that on the bike?" The casement windows of the breakfast room at Castle Moore looked out toward the avenue. Sheila Flaxton squinted over her teacup. "Looks like Torrey Tunet. Maybe bringing the rent for the cottage."

"She mails it," Winifred said. Winifred, fifty years old and big boned, was eating a thickly buttered hard roll and luxuriating in every bite. After growing up poor, an ignored relation, she blissfully enjoyed having inherited Castle Moore two years ago. No more scrabbling for a living. Her prize-winning poetry, much of it published in Sheila Flaxton's well-known *Sisters in Poetry* magazine in London, had paid only a pittance. It still did. But that didn't matter, now that she owned Castle Moore with its six hundred acres of mountains and streams, glens and woods, and its pastures dotted with sheep. Winifred spent the autumn months at Castle Moore, walking the woods, wearing her oversized corduroy jeans and a pullover and taking deep invigorating breaths of the country air. She had a square-jawed face and short reddish gray hair that she wore pushed behind her ears. There was a shrewd look in her gray eyes and a humorous quirk to her mouth.

She said, "Could be that she wants to thank me for sending Dakin Cameron to do some carpentry. Unless she's up to something, as usual. Torrey Tunet never made a simple social call in her life."

"Really, Winifred! You always imagine something hidden in a slice of cake." Sheila warmed her hands around her teacup. She was forty-two, and wispy, with light blue eyes in a somewhat pasty-looking face. She was thin blooded and felt the cold more; this morning she wore two sweaters and a heavy woolen skirt and thick stockings. She had brought a Yugoslavian knitted cap with her from London. Outdoors, she wore it pulled down almost to her eyebrows, covering even her mixed blond and gray fringe.

"Quite right, Sheila. Because there always is." Winifred was watching Torrey bring her bike to a stop at the foot of the steps between the heavy stone balustrades. "*Quite* right. It could be a gold ring. Or a knife."

"Dakin?" Winifred said to Torrey, "Dakin Cameron? Here's the sugar. And take one of the muffins. Rose made them." Rose was the maid who always served breakfast. Winifred poured tea. "Sorry, no coffee. Anyway, Dakin Cameron. Did I mention on the phone that he's on his autumn school holiday? Anyway, he likes carpentry. Built me a supplies cabinet, painted the lodge windowsills. Says he doesn't want his muscles to atrophy. Handsome boy. He'll break hearts. Likely already has. Did a good job for you?"

"Yes. Very. Lives in Ballynagh, does he?"

Winifred laughed. "Oh, you didn't know? He's one of *those* Camerons. The Camerons of Sylvester Hall. He's the son."

"Sylvester Hall?" Torrey blinked, startled. She'd seen photographs of Sylvester Hall and its rolling grounds in glossy magazines. It was a Palladian-style mansion on a distant rise north of the village. The Sylvester estate was one of the largest in western Wicklow.

"I keep forgetting," Winifred said, "You're away so much. So you wouldn't know. Dakin's mother is the beauteous Natalie Sylvester Cameron. She inherited Sylvester Hall from her great-aunt when she was quite young, only twenty. Her parents were killed in an earthquake in the west of Turkey when Natalie was about four. Her great-aunt brought her up. Natalie's now about thirty-eight, thirty-nine."

"*She's* Dakin's mother? Wasn't there something in the news? Some recent, tragic—"

"Right! Two years ago, Natalie's husband, a lawyer, was killed in a cross fire when he was coming out of the Gresham on O'Connell Street. Two drug factions with bad aim."

"My *God*!"

"Yes. It half destroyed Natalie. She adored him. She's a romantic. Looks like one, too: dark, honey-colored hair, hazel eyes under black brows, broad beautiful forehead—that sort of thing."

"Oh? What's she like?"

"A darling. High ideals. Spotless reputation. After her husband was killed, she became involved with affordable housing for low-income families. Thinks it'll help keep drugs away from kids. Ho! Ho! *That'll* be quite a trick!"

"So, Natalie Cameron." Torrey swirled the tea in her cup. Dakin's appalled, startled eyes. Something about his mother.

"Now Natalie's going to marry Marshall West, the architect. The low-cost housing advocate. It was in the papers a couple of weeks ago. He was in Ballynah around then. Dropped into O'Malley's when I was blowing some froth off a blessedly delicious beer, a treat after my six-mile hike. Looks about forty, keen eyes, has a jaw that brooks no nonsense. Reeks of decency, honor, the lot. Left a more-than-respectable tip."

Torrey said, "Uhhuh . . . Thanks for the tea." What she

was looking for, whatever it was, wasn't to be found here at Castle Moore. Waste of time. What *was* she looking for, anyway? She got up. "I'm off."

Winifred speculatively watched Ms. Torrey Tunet pedal off down the avenue. Something doing behind Ms. Tunet's big gray eyes starred by the black lashes.

"Wouldn't you say, Sheila," Winifred said to Sheila Flaxton, "that Ms. Torrey Tunet has that look again?"

"*What* look?"

"Her dragon-slaying look."

"Oh, for heaven's sake, Winifred! You have the most amazing tendency to make something out of nothing."

3

Thursday morning at ten o'clock, Sean O'Boyle finished clipping the boxwood hedges at Sylvester Hall. Shears in hand, he straightened. He was sixty-two. Every Thursday since he was in his thirties, he'd manicured the green lawns that sloped away from the hall down to the woods. He pruned the glossy yews and rhododendrons and cut back the shrubs. In the greenhouse, he planted seeds and nurtured plants. He oversaw the kitchen garden, so there was always a supply of fresh fruits and vegetables for the household. And even after so many years, he still felt a lift of pleasure when his old car rattled through the gates and up the avenue of oaks, and there, set like a gem in the folds of the hills, lay Sylvester Hall.

As for the shears—Sean made a face. They'd gotten dull; he liked a shears sharp as razors. He'd give them a good grinding. The whetstone was kept in the coach house. It was a grindstone that purred like a cat, a pleasure to use; he'd even sharpened his penknife on it. And Breda, the cook, always gave him her kitchen knives to sharpen.

He started across the stone-flagged courtyard toward the handsome coach house. It was grey, with three sets of black, arched double doors, wide enough for carriages with double-harnessed horses. The doors had brass pulls shaped like lions' heads.

But now, of course, it was a garage. There was Ms. Cameron's Saab and Dakin's red Jeep. The old silver Rolls was there, seldom used now, though in Sybil Sylvester's day Olin Caughey, the chauffeur, would drive the old lady to her shopping and bridge games in the Rolls. Not that Olin Caughey should've been driving at all, what with his kidneys always acting up. Tough old bird. "I'll use your guts for garters!" he'd threaten Sean when he'd been drinking. And Sean, younger and stronger, had to laugh.

There was still the one old carriage left in the coach house, though. It was a black boxlike, closed carriage, elegant looking, with two square lamps with beveled glass. A hundred years old. Last year, an antiques fellow had offered Ms. Cameron a hefty sum for the carriage, but she'd turned him down. Odd, because Ms. Cameron wasn't what you'd call sentimental about historical family possessions.

"Mr. O'Boyle?" Jessie Dugan, the younger of the two maids, was coming across the courtyard. She was carrying the morning's post of letters and magazines from the postbox at the end of the avenue.

"Morning, Jessie."

Jessie was frowning, head tipped sideways in puzzlement. "This morning, Mr. O'Boyle—When you got here, did you see anyone about? Maybe near the postbox?"

Sean shook his head.

"Well, *queer*. Yesterday when I got the mail, a letter for Ms. Cameron was in the box without a stamp. Now, this morning, *another* letter! This one." Jessie held up a blue envelope. "Had to've been just *put* there!"

Sean said, offhandedly, "Well, what of that? What with stamps costing as much as a side of bacon to send a letter!" He said it just to have Jessie on. But it *was* odd. In truth, he didn't like it. Anything a bit off sent a little tightness of alarm between his shoulder blades and he'd look about like a deer raising its head at the scent of danger. It always had.

At ten-thirty, after a half hour's brisk morning walk with the two hounds, Natalie Cameron arrived back at Sylvester Hall. She'd been in the woods and fields, nettles clung to her woolen pants. She felt healthy, happy, and glowingly alive; autumn was her season, she loved it.

"Dakin was up at six," Jessie had told her over her late breakfast. "He waited to talk to you. But he finally had to leave. He was putting up scaffolding. The Conklins' barn." Lucinda had left for school at eight.

"Sorry I missed Dakin." She'd been in Dublin until late last night at a meeting about low-cost housing. She'd arrived home after one o'clock and had slept late.

Absentmindedly plucking nettles off her pants, she went into the library. At the big table she settled down and opened the folder of plans for Marshall's housing project. Marshall was somewhere in America. Oregon, a three-week teaching seminar. When he got back, they'd plan the wedding. A dozen close friends. After Andrew's death, she'd thought she'd never be in love again. And why *Marshall*? Forty-two, up from a working-class Scotch-Irish family, and too decent to be true. "Marshall West, the architect," was the way he'd been introduced to her at a fund-raiser. He'd taken her to dinner. He drove a Honda. He had a couple of organic apples in the glove compartment; he liked to munch an apple and listen to music, Beethoven and Mozart. He told her that at nineteen, at university, he'd been engaged, "but my girl suddenly married a soccer player she'd met in a pub the week before." Since then, pleasant, short-lived affairs without true involvement on either side. Until now.

"Ma'am?" Jessie came into the library. "Ma'am? Breda says,

about lunch, Coyle's is out of asparagus, and will broccoli do? She can make the soup with carrots and the broccoli in the blender. And mix in a bit of yogurt for tartness. Considering—"

"Yes, Jessie. Broccoli soup's fine."

"And ma'am?" Jessie glanced at the morning's post that Natalie had picked up from the hall tray but hadn't yet looked through. "That there's another letter without a stamp. The blue. The one on top. If you'll notice."

"Yes, Jessie." Watching Jessie leave, she couldn't help smiling. Jessie, always so apprehensive, as though the sky might fall.

As for that first unstamped letter she'd received Monday morning with its ridiculous enclosure wrapped in a twist of white tissue—! Reading the letter, she'd laughed. What nonsense! A sharp, angular handwriting on copy paper:

A pity to let the exposure of one's past jeopardize one's present life and future! Especially when you're espousing such a worthy cause. Decent housing is critical indeed! I respect your cause! But due to unfortunate circumstances, I am in need of funds. I must save myself. So I have no recourse but to resort to you. In the amount of twenty thousand pounds. At twelve noon on Wednesday, bring twenty thousand pounds to the white cairn cornerstone that separates the Sylvester property from Castle Moore. The Cloverleaf shall then be yours.

Reading the letter Monday morning, she'd been bewildered. Then laughed. Blackmail! Pay up or he—or she?—would expose her past! Was this a joke? Her past? *What* past? How boring that she didn't even *have* a past. She'd never done anything shameful. She was, now that she thought of it, ridiculously moral. True, even as a child she'd had a dirty mouth. But that wasn't a shameful past. "I'm a bloody *paragon*!" she'd said aloud, and laughed.

16

What other foibles? Hung out as a teenager in Dublin pubs, smoking pot? She only wished she had! But from the age of six she'd attended that sickening goody-goody Alcock's Academy, that all-girls school that was strict as a nunnery. Her great-aunt Sybil, who'd brought her up, had seen to that. A tediously numbing experience. Damn it! She'd never even had *time* to do anything worth being blackmailed for!

She'd rattled the preposterous blackmail letter. "You've got the wrong lady!" She'd been barely nineteen when her great-aunt Sybil had taken her on a trip to Italy. In Florence she'd met her beloved Andrew. She'd never cheated on Andrew with a lover. She'd never even been tempted to cheat. After Andrew's death in the cross fire outside the Gresham, she'd had two years of numbness. The children, Dakin and Lucinda, then fourteen and eight, had been her only comfort. Who was the Greek matron who said of her children, "These are my jewels"? Somebody. Penelope? Anyway. Dakin and Lucinda, her jewels. Then four months ago, she'd met Marshall West and fallen in love.

So, incredulously looking down at the letter, she'd laughed. And what did this blackmailer mean by Cloverleaf? *The Cloverleaf shall be yours.* What a crock!

Then, curious, she'd unwrapped the tissue paper. A tarnished silver charm bracelet with three silver unicorns dangling from it. Souvenir-shop kind of cheap bauble. Was it supposed to mean something significant to her? Well, it didn't. She'd tossed it into the wastebasket along with the letter.

But then, frowning, she'd thought, better to keep the letter and its enclosure to show to Inspector O'Hare in case she decided to call him. Such a nuisance! Exasperating. She had a million letters to write about Marshall's housing project. Still . . .

17

She took the letter and charm bracelet from the wastebasket and put them into the shallow desk drawer. Before sliding the drawer closed, she looked down at the bracelet. She frowned. She lifted a hand and brushed her fingers over her left brow as though to brush away something thin and gauzy that obscured her vision. She blinked, and it was gone. She closed the drawer.

Now this second letter.

"Hell and dam*nation*! What a nuisance!" She picked up the blue envelope and slit it open. This second letter, too, had an enclosure wrapped in tissue paper.

Elbows on the desk, exasperated at wasting time over such nonsense, she read the letter, the already-familiar heavy handwriting, with its sharp up-and-down angles:

Same time, Saturday noon. At the white cairn. But now it will cost you thirty thousand pounds. The cloverleaf will be yours.

In place of a signature, a heavy, black dash.

There were two postscripts. The first:

Don't think you can be rid of me until you pay—not even by underhanded means. As for crying out to the law, I've no fear of that, since you're aware that it would lead to the revelation about you—I'd make sure of that. So I am untouchable. As Napoleon said at Montereau, "The bullet that will kill me is not yet cast."

The second postscript said only, "A present for Dakin."

The single sentence made her catch her breath. Dakin. Why Dakin? She tore open the tissue. A small penknife Ivory. Perhaps five inches long.

She sat holding the knife. She turned it over and over. She felt a shiver. The ivory penknife, cool to the touch. Familiar, somehow.

"Ma'am?" Jessie again in the doorway. "Lester's here, to be paid. That's the mulch and the hydrangeas. And he says Sean O'Boyle says plantings are needed along the roadside both sides of the gates, he's given Lester this list."

"You'll find Lester's check on the hall table. Leave the list. Tell him I'll call him tomorrow."

"Yes, ma'am." The door closed behind Jessie.

Familiar. She turned the penknife over and over. Familiar. And then she knew why: Engraved into the ivory on one side were the initials, JHS. Her father's initials. It was the little penknife she'd inherited. It had been her father's as a boy.

She left the library. At the east end of the upper hall, opposite the grandfather clock was the old escritoire. It had been there since her childhood. She'd always thought of it as *her* escritoire, her great-aunt Sybil had had no use for it. She knelt down and opened the base of the grandfather clock. She took out the key to the escritoire. Dust motes rose from inside the clock, making her sneeze.

She unlocked the escritoire. The penknife. She had kept it here in the top left drawer with her other treasured childhood keepsakes.

She pulled open the top drawer. But of course the penknife was not there: she was holding it in her hand. JHS. Her father's ivory penknife. Someone had come into Sylvester Hall and crept up the staircase and stolen the penknife. Who? And why?

A present for Dakin.

4

Ma?" The coach house no longer smelled of horse and feed, but old harnesses still hung from iron hooks. Dakin always thought of sleek horses harnessed to carriages and trotting with arched necks down the avenue. A smell of gasoline now, though, from the cars. Light came only dimly through the high horizontal windows. Dakin walked past the cars to the far end and approached the boxlike old carriage.

"Ma?"

She was in the carriage. He'd suspected she would be. Even as a small boy, he'd known it was her refuge, as though it had some indefinable power, some mysterious means of soothing whatever troubled her.

"It's me." He put a foot on the step and pulled himself up; the springs creaked. He sat down on the faded mulberry-colored button seat opposite his mother. "What's it about?"

"What's *what* about?"

"Don't *you* know?" He was startled. "Yesterday, I was doing some carpentry for a friend of Winifred Moore. That old groundsman's cottage that belongs to Castle Moore? While I was there, I got a phone call, a man's voice. It was a threat. He said, 'Tell your mother to pay attention to the blue envelope communication. If she ignores it, her secret will become public knowledge. Tell her! Everyone will know the truth about her! As for you—' And he laughed. It was too—a nightmare! Out of the blue! It stunned me. When I hung up, he tried to call back. I should have answered, but I couldn't, I was too—too—Is that what shock is like? Bile in one's throat? Sickened?" Dakin leaned toward his mother. "Ma, who's that man? What did he mean? I wanted to kill him!"

His mother said, helplessly, "I've no idea. A man, was it? Anyway, a blackmailer. I want to laugh it off as nonsense. But . . ." She told him then about the two letters and her father's stolen penknife. "That's what bothers me. The penknife. That someone sneaked into Sylvester Hall and stole it. It couldn't have been anybody in the house; Jessie and Breda have worked at the hall for years." She plucked at a frayed bit of the mulberry-colored velvet.

"Ma, you have to call Inspector O'Hare right away. He'll get in touch with Dublin Castle. The crime division will send Gardi to stake out the cairn. When the blackmailer shows up for the money, they'll grab him."

His mother was frowning. "Dakin, I'm thinking. There are people who prey on other people's feelings of guilt. Maybe this Mr. X is one of them. There's that theory that everyone feels guilty about something—or *almost* everybody. Once, to prove it, a psychologist picked ten people's names out of the telephone book and sent them each a telegram saying, 'All has been discovered. Leave town immediately.' Eight of them left town."

"But—"

"*May*be, Dakin, this blackmailer is working on the same principle. Maybe he preys on women! Frightens them into paying him thousands of pounds. So maybe I should just ignore his—"

"Ma. What about your father's penknife?"

His mother stared at him. Then her hazel eyes, so much like his own, wavered. "Yes . . . that." She bit her lips.

"Then you'll call Inspector O'Hare?"

"You're right, Dakin. I'll call O'Hare." But even as she said it, she realized she wasn't going to call O'Hare. It had something to do with . . . with what? She raised her hand and brushed her fingers across her brow; it was as though a gray veil hid something almost glimpsed.

"Good!" Dakin said. "That's that, then."

But because Natalie had never lied to her son, she said, "No, Dakin. I'm not going to call O'Hare. I'm not sure why not. But I won't call him."

Dakin looked at his mother, her ordinarily glowing face had gone pale, her bright hair in the dimness of the carriage had a dull sheen. Against the faded color of the carriage, she looked like some lost Renaissance princess, never mind her sweater and gray pants to which a few nettles still clung.

Dakin said, appalled, "That letter! Saturday noon! You mean you're going to get the money and go to the cairn to meet with this blackmailer?"

"And give him thirty thousand pounds? Of course not! I haven't done anything to warrant this! And what's Clover-leaf? I've no idea." She leaned forward. Her honey-colored hair fell across her brow. "Darling." She laid her hand over the strong, tanned hand that rested on his knee. "I wish you didn't know about any of this."

But he was glad he knew. Because if he hadn't known, there wouldn't have been anything he could do about it.

Dakin gone, she leaned back in the old carriage, soothed as always by its musty-smelling, faded mulberry upholstery. Overtired, that was it, working too hard on the housing project. Otherwise, why this strange little lurching of the heart, as though there was something . . . but how could there be? Yet . . . She raised a hand and brushed it across her eyes. Something glimpsed. Blood oozing on the palm of a hand. *Poor lad*! Laughing, bending her head to lick the palm, the taste of blood. A green . . . box? A marble what? . . . cold to the touch.

"What? *What?*" she said aloud. She gave a jerk as though suddenly roused from sleep. She pushed open the carriage door and stepped out. She was trembling, it was so cold. She should have worn a sweater. It was, after all, October.

5

A few minutes before noon, two hours after Torrey had left Castle Moore, she leaned her bicycle agaainst the wall outside O'Malley's Pub. It wasn't just that she owed Dakin because of the two lads of the fookin' drugs. It was also inherent outrage at the cruel telephone call. So, no use trying to ignore it. *Connaître le dessous des cartes,* as the French had it: know the undersides of the cards. Something in her demanded to know.

There was only a handful of customers in O'Malley's this early. Young Sean was behind the bar cutting cheese into half-inch squares and piling them into bowls and putting out the little glasses of toothpicks. The table at the end of the bar was occupied by Michael McIntyre, its usual occupant at eleven-thirty.

"Mr. McIntyre."

"Ah, the American lass! Sit down! Sit down! A glass or a pint? Have no fear of the bill, 'tis my birthday." Michael McIntyre swiped a hand through his thicket of white hair. He was in his seventies, with a weathered face and brown eyes. He was Wicklow born and at twenty-two had departed Ballynagh for the life of a sailor. But every October, an aging Peter Pan, he returned to Ballynagh. "The village is a drug to me," he'd once told Torrey, "more than a pinch of any powder

24

you'd snuff up your nose in a brothel in Thailand. Thick as a bog with secrets, and I most privy to them all. Many's a quiet little laugh I have up my sleeve." McIntyre knew the ancestry of every cottager, farmer, shop owner, and estate owner in Ballynagh and the foibles and secrets, shameful, laughable, or plain horrendous, of even the most secretive.

"Soup," Torrey said. She sat down. "The Thursday special, lamb and barley." She contemplated McIntyre, who was lifting his pint to take a draft. Whatever she might want to know, she could learn from Michael McIntyre. She knew he liked her, as she liked him; he'd dance about a bit, but he wasn't likely to hold back.

So after she'd taken a few spoonfuls of the lamb and barley, she had only to mention the family at Sylvester Hall. At that, Michael McIntyre studied the ceiling and then the depths of his pint:

"The spinster, Sybil Sylvester, was the last to bear the Sylvester name, but for her great-niece, Natalie. The child, Natalie, had the misfortune to be brought up and guided into pure womanhood by Ms. Sybil." McIntyre drained his pint and held up the glass, signaling to young Sean behind the bar. Sean nodded and said a word to his sister Emily, the barmaid.

"Misfortune?"

"Indeed, indeed! A barrelful of that." McIntyre raised a hand and gave another stir to his mass of unruly hair. "The spinster, Sybil Sylvester, looked a jolly little person, a buttercup, a daisy, twinkly blue eyes, rosebud mouth. Porcelain figurine seen in a souvenir shop window. Had a fiancé and marriage all arranged for her, but he was killed in the war. They say she was relieved because his estate had shrunk. Bad management and a fire. Hah! Then, as the finger of destiny decreed, her nephew, Natalie's father, along with her mother, disposed of by an earthquake—on terra firma of course. And they say the sea's a devil!" McIntyre gave a snort of a laugh.

"So Ms. Sybil was left in command. And with the child to bring up. According to her lights."

Torrey stirred her soup. "And what lights were those, Mr. McIntyre?"

"Disciplinary lights! In the extreme. As for the rest, all well ordered: Sybil Sylvester spent her days running Sylvester Hall and its farmlands with a gimlet eye. Evenings, stiff dinners, black tie, or playing bridge with ladies and gentlemen of equally exalted family backgrounds. No Catholics allowed. Thank you, Emily." McIntyre picked up the pint that Emily set down before him.

Torrey said, cautiously, "But you mean, about discipline 'in the extreme,' about handling her responsibility to the child, Natalie—"

"Hah!" McIntyre set his pint down so hard that the beer splashed on the table: "A child, desperate, trying to swim in a tight corset! Underwater, drowning, tearing at the laces. Frantic! I saw it, and I thought, God knows what it can lead to!" McIntyre's voice was hoarse with emotion. Then the lids of his dark eyes flicked in a way that Torrey recognized: the curtain coming down.

McIntyre said, "In the Aleutian Islands—I was thirty-two then. That November the *Octavia* ran into a storm. The sea became wild, waves high as mountains, the *Octavia* began wallowing. . . ."

So that was all, for now. Bewildering. A very slender thread to that threatening phone call.

6

Dakin couldn't help it. Like now, looking down at Kate Burnside lying there in the tumble of bedclothes on the divan in O'Sullivan's barn. She was still asleep though it was already noon, and she was surely drunk, her full-lipped mouth a little open. Whenever he saw Kate, he got all heavy breathing and would think of silk or satin, some sliding, slippery material. Kate was his mother's age, maybe a year younger.

Divan. That's what Kate called the bed. It was like a wide couch, "Persian," she'd told him, "sultans slept on divans. Potentates with their concubines." She kept her paints and a jumble of her expensive clothes in O'Sullivan's barn, it was her studio. Her paintings, splashy abstracts that didn't sell, leaned against the walls. In Dublin she had an elegant town house.

"Kate! Wake up! Come on!" He bent over and shook her shoulder. He needed her help. Almost from babyhood Kate and his mother had attended Alcock's Academy and been best friends. True, his mother and Kate had drifted apart years ago. Their lives had become too different. Kate had had two notorious divorces, her children lived with their fathers. Her friends were fellow painters, men who were, it was said, often her lovers.

27

"Kate! Come on! wake up!"

Kate's eyes opened. She squinted at Dakin, then yawned so widely that her eyes teared. She stretched. She said lazily, "Dakin! You dear thing. I'm thrilled to see you. My mouth is an absolute—I could use some orange juice. And make some coffee. Use the filter thing. It's on the drainboard."

"So," Dakin said, "she's had these two letters." He hunched forward on the hassock beside the divan and ran a finger around the rim of his coffee cup. He'd taken off his parka and was wearing a long-sleeved jersey. The studio was warmed by a peat fire in a cast-iron stove, yet he gave a sudden shiver. "What's so crazy is that my mother doesn't even know what the blackmailer's talking about. She's perplexed. But she refuses to go to Inspector O'Hare! Why not? She doesn't even seem to *know* why not! She just acted somehow . . . *off somewhere*." He could see his mother across from him in the coach, he saw her raise her hand and her slender fingers brush in front of a hazel eye. "Off somewhere," he repeated. Edgy, he ran a hand through his hair.

Kate, cross-legged on the divan in a pink satin nightgown with a bit of torn tan lace on one shoulder, was holding her coffee cup in both hands, and watching him.

He leaned forward. "Kate, d'you remember anything that happened? That this blackmailer could've misconstrued?"

"No! Nothing!" Kate sounded so irritable that Dakin was startled. "You're assuming the blackmail's about something that happened years ago. Maybe Natalie made some financial transaction a year or two ago that wasn't exactly on the up-and-up. A profitable, and not-quite-legal bit of—"

"My *mother*?" Dakin gave an incredulous laugh. "Not on your life! And there's that about her father's penknife, it must've been stolen. And what's it supposed to signify to my mother? *She* doesn't know. She's in the dark. She—" He stopped. Funny, the way Kate was looking at him, not seeing him all of a sudden. Then she gave herself a little shake. She put her coffee cup down on the end table. She pulled her long black hair back in a ponytail and snapped a rubber band around it. Her white-lidded brown eyes were heavy and reddened. "Poor Natalie! What's she going to do? Will she go to meet this blackmailer on Saturday? Or not? Don't keep me waiting with bated breath."

Dakin said tightly, "I thought I said. No. She won't. She's not giving any phony blackmailer even one pound. She says she's done nothing to warrant being blackmailed. Nothing."

Kate drained her coffee cup, then put it down and got up from the divan. Barefoot, slender, and full-breasted, the pink satin nightgown falling off one shoulder, she wandered to the bookcase against the far wall. She ran her fingers slowly over a row of books. She said, lazily, "I'm in a mood to read. Maybe *The Brothers Karamazov*. Or *Remembrance of Things Past*. Something in the French or Russian style."

Dakin sighed. He felt heavy, burdened. A waste of time, coming to Kate Burnside. What, after all, could she know that might help?

And here she was, coming back, coming up behind him where he sat on the hassock, he felt her warm bare arms sliding along the sides of his neck and then her breasts pressing against his back, and he breathed in her bed warmth, and he thought, Yes, again, like last time and the time before and before that, ever since he was fourteen. Kate. Kate.

7

On Saturday, by noon the sun had warmed the meadows, so that a pungent smell of earth rose from the ground. From the east meadow, past the tumbled stone fence and the stand of oaks that separated Castle Moore property from the west field of Sylvester Hall, came the mooing of cows. Crickets chirped, birds sang.

Waiting, he smoked a cigarette. Then he leaned back against a leafy oak beside the cairn. He had no loss of confidence. She'd come. She'd wasted his time, holding off paying. Still, he'd be the richer for it.

There, now! A flutter of white over there beyond the ridge of trees. He glimpsed her approaching figure; she wore a long white skirt with black boots and a close-fitting tan sweater.

Triumphant, he folded his arms and waited. She came across the meadow to where he stood. She came within a few feet of him and stopped. She stared at him. Her eyes grew wide.

"The money." he said curtly.

Brown eyes, heavy-lidded, just staring. Then she laughed. "But you're not — You're not . . ."

"The money!" he repeated impatiently, looking back at her. His gaze slid down from her face. The tan sweater had a V-neck, he saw the cleft of her breasts that glistened a little with dampness; she must have hurried. Her hair was long and dark and drawn back carelessly into a ponytail, so that wisps floated free. And looking at her, he remembered a dim photograph and then he knew that this woman was not Natalie Cameron.

The woman was looking back at him, a puzzled and half-smiling look; but now she raised a hand and touched her lower lip, and in her gaze was something else he recognized, and he began to feel a growing throb in his groin, an exciting ache. Whoever this woman was and why she had come he had to know. But he also had a familiar, greedy feeling that demanded satiety.

8

Luce Cameron was ten. For a week now, she'd had head lice, which was why she wore her brimmed cap all day, even in school. There was the gel-like ointment her mother had twice so far to comb in and wash out, and the cap had to be washed every day too. The gel was that new stuff that didn't smell bad, more like herbs, but everybody knew that new-stuff smell. "It's so em*barr*assing," she said to Dakin almost every day, "as though we live in squalid circumstances. At least it's Saturday, so I don't have to go."

Instead, she'd play in the woods.

She left Sylvester Hall close to noon. Breda had made her a cold beef sandwich. She'd brought her magnifying glass in case she decided to study ants. She'd seen a movie in Dunlavin, it had horses and a beautiful countryside and a naked man pulling his pants on in a hurry when the husband came back from fox hunting and opened the bedroom door. But the interesting part was about ants. The red ants raiding the black ants and kidnapping their children to take home as slaves. Or maybe it was the black ants raiding the red ones?

But all that was, as Dakin would have said, *academic*, because by noontime she hadn't seen a single anthill. Or ant. Autumn must be the wrong season.

Autumn was beautiful, though. In the distance she saw

Castle Moore. It looked so romantic, though it really had only the one turret left and needed all kinds of repairs that Winifred Moore said she wouldn't spend a single pound on.

In the sunny west meadow, Luce found a rock big enough to sit on. She took the sandwich from her backpack and unwrapped it. Nothing could be more perfect than sitting here in the sun eating a beef-and-mustard and with the little bottle of orange pop. And hearing the birds singing, and the rustle of small game, and—someone laughing. Tinkly laughter, coming from somewhere. And again.

Luce settled her cap and tipped her head down a little to keep the sun from her eyes. The laughter, again. A woman's laugh. From off there by the oaks.

And then, as she told herself later, she wasn't spying. It was just that she happened to be there near the cairn.

9

The Sunday lunchtime special at O'Malley's Pub was steak, peas, and mashed potatoes. At one o'clock, Torrey was forking up the last delicious mouthful when the stranger came in.

Torrey did not at first notice him. The barroom was crowded and she was sitting beyond the bar at one of the smaller round tables back near the fireplace. There was low chatter and the smell of beers and grilled meats and the warmth of the fire.

Eating the Sunday lunch, she was pleased with herself. She'd read both of the short Simenon novels with surprising ease, even though an amazing number of Hungarian words were startlingly different from the same words in the other basic twenty-six languages. Nouns in the other languages were all similar, even the Russian. *Night*, for instance. *Office*. *Passport*. Even *pharmacy*. But Hungarian was another kettle of nouns, entirely. Worth exploring the *why* of it. Also, she'd had an E-mail from Myra Schwartz at Interpreters International in Boston. In November, a weeklong job in Lisbon lined up. International trade. "They asked specifically for you, like last year," Myra wrote. "The Portuguese were impressed, they said you even got their in jokes."

Torrey had grinned at that, pleased. Interpreting was a risky business with fallow periods, you never knew. She lived on the edge, with a fluctuating bank account. It was like skiing close to a precipice, yet at the last perilous instant twisting away. Exhilarating, though. She loved it. And she had just banked her check for the European Union meeting in Prague. She had a chance to relax now, before the assignment in Budapest. Maybe she'd buy a nubby corduroy material and cover the shabby old couch in the kitchen.

Yet. Yet this last day or two, she'd become restless, gazing out of the kitchen window to where she'd seen the glint of dying sunlight shining on . . . what? binoculars? and the phone had rung for Dakin.

Hungry, these last couple of days, she couldn't seem to settle down and cook anything. She wandered about the cottage eating chocolate bars with almonds. None of the groceries she'd bought in Ballynagh tempted her. This morning, she'd stood with folded arms looking at the cans of tuna fish in the kitchen cabinet. Rice. Dried milk. A shaker of grated cheese. Out of these, Jasper could've made a mouthwatering masterpiece. She could not.

But at least Dakin Cameron had appeared on Thursday afternoon at four o'clock, as he'd promised. He'd expertly framed the window and now it was snug, no drafts. Torrey hadn't mentioned Wednesday's threatening phone call. Something about the set of Dakin's shoulders warned her not to. Despite the chilly afternoon, he shed his jacket after working for a half hour. Underneath he was wearing one of his mustard-colored jerseys. This one had a bushy-tailed squirrel printed on the chest. The jersey he'd worn the day before had had a turtle imprint. Maybe he was an animal lover? Or liked that mustard color? She didn't ask.

But one thing she did ask was why he did odd jobs around Ballynagh. "Why *do* you?" she'd asked him, admittedly indelicately when, after he'd been working an hour, she'd brought him out a mug of hot cider. Dakin had flushed. "I like to.

And, well . . . My father would've laughed and been glad of it. We're alike, my father and I. 'Inherited riches is just luck,' he once told me, 'Let's see your real baggage.' "

In O'Malley's, a sudden blast of music from the television set above the bar. Jack, the younger O'Malley boy, quickly turned it down, apologetically lifting his shoulders. Standing at the bar almost beneath the television screen, Torrey saw the man she'd noticed come into O'Malley's some minutes ago. What now registered with her was that he wore city clothes: a dark suit with a gray shirt and striped blue-and-gray tie. There were always a few strangers in Ballynagh at any season—tourists in country tweeds; weekenders come for the fishing in the streams that rushed down from the mountains; hikers, booted and jacketed, who stayed a weekend or overnight at Nolan's Bed and Breakfast. But the only place that city folks, those in suits and ties, were likely to be seen in Ballynagh was on television.

The stranger had an untouched pint before him on the bar. He was perhaps in his forties. He was dark haired and good looking, with a narrow, pale face. His brows were drawn together and he had an impatient, angry look. Just now, he was pulling at his striped tie, pulling it this way and that, as though it were choking him. Suddenly he slammed a fist down on the bar, threw down some coins, and was gone.

"Here you are, Ms. Tunet." Emily put Torrey's change on the table.

"Thanks, Emily." Sorting out a tip, and then fitting the pound notes into her wallet, Torrey was thinking: a stranger, neither hunter, fisherman, nor vacationing tourist. By the oak near the cottage, the cigarette butt.

She got up so abruptly that the chair legs scraped noisely on the floor.

10

"It was a few minutes after one o'clock," as Torrey later that afternoon told Inspector O'Hare. By that time, there were bramble scratches on her forehead and bloodstains on the knees of her khaki pants.

Coming out of O'Malley's, she saw the stranger heading up toward the road north of the village. He had a long stride. She hesitated. Was she being ridiculous? Too imaginative? Oh, go ahead! Nothing to lose. She got on her bike.

At that instant she felt her arm gripped. "Ms. Tunet! Hello, Hello!" A deep, hearty voice. "Lucky, running into you!" It was Winifred Moore, on her head a suede Robin Hood sort of hat and wearing leggings, over her twill pants. "Having a poetry reading at St. Andrew's next Sunday. From my new book, *Slivers of Womanhood*. Four o'clock. I'm hoping you can—"

"Yes, absolutely, I'd love to. Four o'clock, right?" She looked after the stranger. He had reached the end of the street and was crossing the stone bridge over the stream. Behind him, several village women were trudging along, chatting, laughing, their laughter floating back. Two of the women, between them, were carrying a couch. They must be heading home from the Sunday jumble sale behind Duffy's garage. There were cottages and farms off the main road beyond the bridge.

"See you later, then!" She pushed off. The cobbled street made her bicycle wheels wobble. Twice the wheels twisted and she fell off. She gave up and walked the bike fast until she reached the bridge where the graveled road began.

Back on the bike, she pedaled on, looking ahead, but the road curved sharply to her left, and when she rounded it she almost ran into the two women carrying the couch. "Watch out, miss!" Indignant faces. "Sorry," Torrey said, "Sorry." "Well, just a minute, then, miss." The women edged the couch around to a rutted road; beyond, smoke rose from a cottage chimney. "A beauty, isn't it?" one of the women said, friendly. "Got it for eight pounds! Worth a hundred. Used to belong to Nellie Egan's mother that passed away. Eight pounds!" "Yes, well, good luck." Torrey edged around and was off on the Peugeot. What next? A herd of elephants in the middle of the road? With a feeling of urgency, she rounded a curve and saw in disappointment that she was too late, even the rest of the women had disappeared, going down paths and roads to their cottages. She slowed the bike. What was the difference, anyway? The man was just another tourist, she'd gotten the wind up about nothing, she was being ridiculous. Give up. Turn back. Go home. Get the Budapest daily newspapers on the Internet, there were always words, expressions, that were used in new, slangy ways.

Still . . . the road ahead was the kind of narrow Irish country road she loved. There were high hedges on either side. Behind them would be farms with broad fields. So, carpe diem. At least a half hour of breathing in the crisp, green-smelling air, and from a cottage somewhere, a whiff of wood smoke. Feet again on the pedals, she pushed off.

Barely a mile beyond, the hedges on her left gave way to meadows where cattle grazed. On her right was a birch wood. Sylvan. From the Latin, meaning "wood." She thought of Thoreau and bicycled blissfully on. Branches of roadside elms shaded the road. A weedy stream flowed alongside the road and disappeared into the woods; small animals rustled in the autumn leaves; there was the flutter of birds' wings.

Then on her right, behind briars, and running along the side of the road, she saw a tall, wrought-iron fence, its rails topped with iron fleur-de-lis. She remembered then the magazine photographs of Sylvester Hall with its wrought-iron fence and stately gates. Were the gates on this road? Curiosity nagged. She'd push on, but only around the next curve. Then back to Ballynagh.

A jolt, as the Peugeot's front wheel struck a pothole, and her pocket radio in the bicycle basket exploded into "Mack the Knife." Louis Armstrong.

Damn it! That loose connection again. She fumbled the radio out from under her extra sweater in the basket and pressed the off button. The music stopped.

So, then, around that next curve. Then back to Ballynagh. She pushed off. Thirty feet ahead, she rounded the curve.

"Help! Help!" A woman in an olive green coat was stumbling along the road toward her, crying out. Torrey skidded the bike to a stop. The woman was panting, her eyes were wide with fright. "I *saw!* A man! He was sneaking up behind the fellow—I *saw* it! I was taking a walk, and—oh, *God!* He must have killed him! Get the police! Get the *police!*"

The woman reached out and clutched the bicycle's handlebars. She was a plump, blond woman with an American accent. Her eyes were wide with shock. She turned her head from Torrey and looked back toward a clump of bushes beside tall wrought-iron gates. "*There,*" she managed.

Torrey slid off the bike. Going toward the bushes, she

39

could hear the woman whimpering behind her. The bushes were prickly and tore at her hair as she knelt beside the man's body. He lay on his side, blood oozing from his forehead and sliding down his temple into the grass. His eyes were half-open, unseeing slits in his narrow, pale face.

He was the stranger Torrey had seen in O'Malley's, the man in the dark suit and striped tie.

The American woman was at Torrey's shoulder. "He could be *dead*! The fellow who attacked him saw me! Then he must have heard someone coming! Jazz music! He ran through the gates and up the avenue!" Her voice was shrill with hysteria.

The man on the ground made a sound in his throat, a thin rasp.

"He's not dead, that's sure." Torrey said. "I'll get help." She stood up and looked around. A boy and girl, teenagers, had come from farther up the road. They were looking curiously at Torrey and at the American woman who had her fists pressed against her cheeks.

Torrey saw with relief that the iron gates of Sylvester Hall were open. "Stay with her!" she called to the boy and girl, and ran up the avenue.

11

The sun had clouded over. The ambulance from Glasshill thirty miles away came to a stop beside the Ballynagh police car.

"Over there," Inspector Egan O'Hare said to the two white-clad attendants who jumped from the ambulance. He jerked his head toward the body that lay in the brambles beside the iron gates of Sylvester Hall.

O'Hare, a heavy-set, keen-eyed man in his early fifties, stood with hands clasped behind his back and feet apart, a habitual pose. He looked from under his brows at the four people who stood watching: the pair of teenagers who were wide-eyed and silent; the woman in an olive green coat who was whimpering; and—God help him!—Ms. Torrey Tunet. Inspector O'Hare couldn't quite suppress a groan. Beside him, Sergeant Jimmy Bryson, aware, managed not to grin.

"Gently, *gently*!" O'Hare said to the younger ambulance attendant, who stumbled on the briars and let the stretcher tip, so that the unconscious man's body strained against the buckled straps. A dried trickle of blood ran from the man's temple down one side of his cheek; his temple was already swelling, the blow must have been near lethal. A stranger. A tourist? Alive, thank God! Even so, a murderous attack.

Hardly an advert for Ballynagh. Not that the village was anyway a mecca for tourists.

The attendants slid the stretcher into the ambulance. Sergeant Jimmy Bryson, whistling under his breath, was bending over and scanning the brambled area where the man's body had lain.

"The *attacker*! He *saw* me!" the American woman in the green coat wailed. Her face was pale with fright, possibly even shock.

"Yes, well," O'Hare said. He'd want statements, the sooner the better, the attack still fresh in their minds. There'd be room enough in the police car for the two teenagers and this agitated witness. As for Ms. Tunet, she had her bicycle and she knew too damned well where the Ballynagh police station was; even if she were on Mars and blindfolded, she would find her way there, and Nelson, tail wagging, would slobber all over her, for God's sake.

Inspector O'Hare shook his head.

Standing beside her bicycle, Torrey watched the police car disappear up the road. Then she turned the bicycle and pedaled fast through the iron gates and up the avenue to Sylvester Hall.

Jessie, the second maid, opened the door. "Ms. Cameron's waiting in the library." She led the way through the great cream-and-blue hall with its rotunda ceiling.

The library was in the west wing. Natalie Cameron in tan wool pants and a brown crew-necked sweater was sitting on a window seat, gazing out and biting a fingernail. She looked around, smiled at Torrey, and got up. "Hello, again. I saw them leave—the ambulance, and the rest. Thanks for coming back." She had a low, husky voice, oddly appealing. "What I wanted to ask you—Dakin told me that he did some carpentry for you at your cottage last Wednesday. Late afternoon? I . . ." She faltered, stopped.

"Yes?" Torrey gazed at Dakin's mother. As Winifred Moore had said, Natalie Cameron was a beauty. Hair the color of dark honey grew low on her brow, which was wide, with a clear look. She had hazel eyes framed by straight, almost black eyebrows, a startling effect. Her nose was bluntly rounded and her mouth was full-lipped. She was probably thirty-five or thirty-six. Right now, she looked anxious.

"It *seems*," Natalie Cameron said, "that while Dakin was doing the carpentry, he got a rather odd phone call. An unknown person, threatening—Dakin said that you tried to help? Spoke to the caller?" Her husky voice quavered.

"Yes. I just, on impulse—"

"So *strange*! Upsetting." Nervously, Natalie Cameron pushed up her sweater sleeves. "Or someone's idea of a lark?" She cast a sideways look at Torrey.

"I don't think so," Torrey said. "It was a cold voice, a man's. In command. Something familiar, though, an accent— I couldn't quite place it." But she would; it would come to her, she'd recognize it, it only took time. She watched Natalie Cameron push her sweater sleeves up and down. "I wish I could help."

"Oh, it's nothing!" Natalie Cameron said quickly, "Likely just some dreadful, nasty joke. Maybe to upset Dakin, one of his school friends managing to fake an adult voice."

Why wasn't Natalie Cameron admitting it? She was troubled far more than a nasty joke warranted. Torrey said, "Well, they succeeded. He *was* upset." But she was staring at Natalie Cameron's left inner arm where the soft white flesh was marred by a puckered scar that ran halfway down to her wrist.

"Oh!" Natalie Cameron caught her glance and quickly

pulled down her sweater sleeve. "Awful, isn't it? So ugly. I was in an auto accident. Ages ago, in Dublin. That was my only scar. But the accident shook me up badly." She laughed suddenly. "The lucky part was that my great-aunt took me abroad to recover. In Italy, in Florence, we stayed at a pensione where I met Andrew Cameron. I was nineteen, he was twenty-six. We fell instantly in love. Isn't it amazing how an unfortunate little accident can result in something marvelous?"

12

At the glass-fronted police station on Butler Street, Sergeant Jimmy Bryson, feeling alive and keen, "in action" as he thought of it, fixed a cup of tea for the American woman. She sat rigidly in the "good" chair—the one with arms—beside Inspector O'Hare's desk. She was trying to comb her short, rather frizzy blond hair with her fingers. It was already four o'clock.

The two teenagers sat over beside the soda machine, sipping cans of Coke. Nelson, Inspector O'Hare's black Lab, rested his head on the boy's knee and slowly wagged his tail. "Forget it," the boy said, "it'll rot your teeth."

O'Hare, at his desk, waited until the woman had a chance to take a few sips of the hot tea. Meanwhile, he took a new cassette from the bottom drawer of his desk, put it into the recording machine, and made sure the machine was working, because sometimes it wasn't. "Now, Ms. —?"

"Plant. Brenda Plant." The woman's voice was shaky, but a little color had come back to her face. Pale blue eyes beneath sandy brows, a nondescript nose that was now faintly red with cold. A wide, thin-lipped mouth. Her frizzy blond hair was cut below her ears and stood out in what O'Hare thought of as a Dutch bob, though he wasn't sure precisely what that was. He made circles on a pad, while she talked.

Brenda Plant, a widow, aged forty, an interior decorator from Buffalo, New York. On her way to an all-Irish antiques convention in Cork. She'd arrived in Ballynagh at eleven o'clock this morning in a Honda rented at the Dublin airport and had booked into Nolan's Bed and Breakfast for a stay of five days to visit antique shops in the area before continuing on to Cork. She'd lunched at Miss Amelia's Tea Shoppe. Then she'd thought, a nice walk up that "marvelously rustic road." There'd been a few other women on the road, going home from some sort of church jumble sale, but they'd dropped off, one after another, going up this or that dirt path or road. Alone, she'd strolled on, enjoying the countryside, when, having rounded a curve —

"I saw a man . . . the *vic*tim. He was sitting on a rock by the side of the road. He was just sitting there, looking toward big iron gates that opened onto an avenue." Then up behind him had come another man. "He raised a stick — it was thick as a club! — and brought it down on the man's head. I cried out! I was so *horr*ified. He heard me. He looked over. He *saw* me! Then he ran up through the gates." Ms. Plant dragged her fingers distractedly through her permed hair and looked back at Inspector O'Hare. Her light blue eyes, with mascara that had run a bit, were anxious. She shivered and pulled the collar of her coat more closely around her neck.

"The man," O'Hare said, "what did he look like?"

"I couldn't exactly — He had on one of those fishing hats with the brim down all around. So I couldn't exactly — But I know he *saw* me! And of course *heard* me!"

"Nothing to worry about now, Ms. Plant," O'Hare said. "The man who was attacked will likely regain consciousness soon. You might be of further help. Needless to say, we'll appreciate your cooperation."

46

Ms. Plant looked doubtful. "Oh, well, yes. If there's anything . . ."

When the door closed behind Ms. Plant, O'Hare looked over at the two teenagers beside the soda machine. Willie Hern was the boy, and that was his girlfriend, Marcy, Henry McGann's oldest. Now let's see what *they'd* witnessed.

As for that final witness, the annoying, meddlesome Ms. Torrey Tunet, that pebble in his shoe—where was she? Exasperating young woman. Looked a straight-backed proper young cadet, never mind the ruffled, short dark hair and that "mouth like a flower" as old Michael McIntyre described it. Probably snooping around the Sylvester Hall gates, and she'd drift in when ready, indolent, hands in the pockets of her jeans. Knowing more than she should, as usual, and keeping it buttoned up.

O'Hare hissed out a breath. Meantime, who was the stranger who now lay unconscious in the twelve-bed Glasshill Hospital?

Inspector O'Hare picked up the man's expensive-looking lizardskin wallet and opened it.

13

At eight o'clock Monday morning, Winifred Moore, smartly dressed in pants, white shirt, and tweed jacket was sopping up the last bit of yolk from her fried eggs in the breakfast room at Castle Moore when Sheila appeared, still in her dressing gown.

"Winifred!"

"Not *dressed* yet?" Winifred said, exasperated. "Oh, God! We'll get a late start! The horses will have died of old age, much less finished jumping."

"You've got jam on your mouth, Winifred. The left corner. *Well!* I was listening to the early morning news while I was brushing my teeth. And can you be*lieve* it! A man was attacked yesterday right here in Ballynagh! Bludgeoned! Almost *killed*! Nobody knows who did it, a woman actually *saw it happening* and—"

"Bludgeoned," Winifred said. "I like that word. Bludgeoned. Sometimes, one gets so caught up in the current bland idiom that one forgets—Who was he? Where in Ballynagh? What happened?"

"That road that goes past Sylvester Hall? It was just outside the gates to Sylvester Hall. A Canadian, apparently a tourist, was attacked. Mr. Thomas Brannigan, from Montreal. Bashed, bludgeoned. Luckily, Ms. Torrey Tunet, a resident of Ballynagh happened to be—"

"Ah, yes," Winifred said, "Ms. Torrey Tunet. Naturally. I would have guessed it."

14

At noontime on Monday, Finney's, across the street from the police station, celebrated its forty-fifth year in business by serving a chops-licking noontime feast. O'Hare had the roast lamb with an edging of crisp fat, green beans, and mashed potatoes. Dessert was on the house, and O'Hare had the strawberry-rhubarb pie. Two pieces. That flaky crust. Nobody could make a crust like Finney's wife, Mary.

But now, at three o'clock when the door to the police station opened and O'Hare looked up from his desk to see Torrey Tunet, he felt a sharp stab of indigestion. The roast lamb? The two pieces of pie? Exasperation?

"Afternoon, Inspector." Ms. Tunet had a low, clear voice. "I came because there's something I forgot to mention to you yesterday. About that fellow who was attacked?" Ms. Tunet smiled at him. She had that peacock bandana snug around her short, wavy dark hair and the October wind had made her cheeks red. She wore a thick brown sweater and tan dungerees tucked into brogues. Above all, she looked exhilarated. Snooping about. Meat and drink to her. Why couldn't she stick to her translating? No, that wasn't the right word. *Interpreting*, that was it.

"Did you, now?" *Forgot*? Lying, of course. Sticking her nose in where it wasn't wanted. He was fifty-four and had been inspector in Ballynagh for twenty-two years. There were times when he sensed things as though an inner ear were receiving messages. He wished to hell that Ms. Tunet were not involved. This was *his* show. He couldn't help that he bitterly resented that a year ago she'd saved his reputation with the Garda Síochána, the national police force headquartered at Phoenix Park in Dublin. Saved his neck with Chief Superintendent O'Reilley, what with her knowledge of foreign tongues, so that at the crucial moment— Blast it! He couldn't help the resentment. "Yes?" He drew a notebook closer and picked a pen out of the mug of pens and pencils on the desk. He twiddled the pen and waited, looking at Ms. Tunet.

"That Canadian? Brannigan?" Ms. Tunet said, "He came into O'Malley's at lunchtime yesterday, about one o'clock. He was there maybe . . . oh, ten, fifteen minutes. At the bar. Then he went out. In a rage." She stopped. O'Hare waited. Not a word more. "That's *it*?" He put down the pen. "That's *all*?"

"Hmmm?" Ms. Tunet wasn't listening. She was looking at the Aer Lingus flight bag on O'Hare's desk, the bag that Sergeant Bryson had brought from Nolan's Bed and Breakfast last night. She was looking at the Canadian passport on the desk. As for herself, she looked as immovable as a Stonehenge monolith.

O'Hare gave up. It would anyway be in the *Dublin Times* and the *Independent* tomorrow morning. Maybe down in a corner of a back page, it was not big news. He opened the folder on his desk and settled his glasses:

"Thomas P. Brannigan, Montreal, Canada. Aged thirty-eight. Birthplace: Drumcliff, County Sligo, Ireland." He looked up. "County Sligo's in the northwest."

"I know *that*," Ms. Tunet said.

There was a sudden hum from over on Sergeant Bryson's

desk. A paper slowly began to emerge from the fax machine. Nelson wagged his tail at the machine. Inspector O'Hare got up. Standing over the fax machine, he waited. Ms. Tunet stood beside him whistling "The Lion Sleeps Tonight" under her breath. O'Hare suppressed a sigh of exasperation. The fax machine stopped and he impatiently twitched the fax from the machine. It bore the letterhead of the Montreal Police Department.

Back at his desk, O'Hare grudgingly read the message aloud; Ms. Tunet at least had the good grace to stand on the other side of the desk, rather than peering over his shoulder:

" 'Thomas B. Brannigan. No arrests or convictions. Unmarried. Graduate of McGill University. Owns and runs The Citadel, an upscale bookshop on Ste. Catherine Street. Member of Foursquare Literary Club. Recipient of this year's Halsey Prize for a volume of poetry.' "

The door opened; the wind slammed it shut behind Sergeant Jimmy Bryson. "Bitch of a wind," Bryson said, then noticed Torrey Tunet beside O'Hare's desk. He blushed. He never used bad language before women. He was twenty-four, played soccer in O'Shaugnessy's field on Sunday mornings, dated Hannah, who worked at Castle Moore, and loved his life, complete with his blue garda uniform, and a bit of action like now. An ambulance siren stirred his blood. Real things happening.

"All set with Ms. Plant," he said to O'Hare, "Sara Hobbs will keep an eye out." Sara Hobbs, who with her husband, Brian, owned Nolan's Bed and Breakfast, was related to Jimmy on his mother's side, so he'd had a bit of luck there. Sara had moved Brenda Plant into the room adjoining her own. "I'm right there and a light sleeper," Sara had reassured Ms. Plant, who seemed a little nervous after her upsetting experience.

"Fine, Jimmy, fine," O'Hare said. He looked a frowning

good-bye at Ms. Tunet, but she just put her hands in her pockets and smiled at Sergeant Bryson, who said, "What I was thinking, Inspector — It would be nice if I took Ms. Plant to Finney's for supper tonight, like under the auspicies of the Ballynagh Police Department? Considering."

O'Hare frowned. The budget was small.

"Shepherd's pie tonight," Sergeant Bryson said, "and considering her cooperation, and the unfortunate — Anyway, she'll be leaving in a couple of days, the antiques show in Cork. So I was thinking —"

"Fine! Fine!" O'Hare frowned, annoyed that Ms. Tunet was standing there, listening. A thorn in his side. This was police business. Confidential.

"I'm going." Ms. Tunet went to the door, then she turned. "If there's any way I can help —"

Not even if I had burning straws under my fingernails. Inspector O'Hare refrained from saying it aloud. Instead, he nodded. "Certainly, Ms. Tunet."

But she hadn't yet gone: "I was wondering — those teenagers? Willie Hern and Marcy McGann. Did they see anything of the attack?"

"Nothing." O'Hare put up a hand and gently probed below his breastbone. It was definitely not the two pieces of pie. It was the nosiness of Ms. Torrey Tunet. "Unfortunately, they came walking up the road too late to see anything."

"Well, a shame." The wind slammed the door shut behind Ms. Tunet.

15

Torrey braked her bike to a stop at the gates of Sylvester Hall and got off. She stood looking about. Yesterday, Marcy McGann and Willie Hern had told Inspector O'Hare that they hadn't seen anything of the attack. They'd been coming from the opposite direction, from the McGann farm, which lay a half mile beyond Sylvester Hall.

Torrey walked toward the bushes beside the iron gates. She ought to give Inspector O'Hare credit for a thorough investigation. But the fact was, she didn't. Maybe there was something that O'Hare and Sergeant Jimmy Bryson had missed. Maybe something in that clump of bushes where Thomas Brannigan had fallen when he'd been struck down. Easy enough to have overlooked something.

The bushes were low and straggly along the roadside. In her brogues, Torrey tread carefully, peering down, eyes narrowed. There were pebbles and stones and bits of road debris and dried bits of dead branches and leaves. Nothing more. Give up, forget it.

An odd, shivery sensation. Someone was there, stone still, watching her. She looked around. On the other side of gates was a figure. After an instant, Torrey gave a laugh, relieved. It was only Sean O'Boyle!

"Mr. O'Boyle! He*llo*!" Sean O'Boyle. Torrey knew he did

the landscaping at Sylvester Hall. He tended the flower beds and the shrubberies, he kept the avenue weeded, he babied seedlings in the greenhouse and oversaw the kitchen garden. Dependable. A quiet man. Hardly ever opened his mouth, but for a Good day or Good evening, unless he was talking about plants.

"Morning, Ms. Tunet."

Torrey came closer to the gates. Sean O'Boyle was holding a tape measure, the retractable steel kind. He must have seen her curiosity. "Bushes alongside the gates," he said. "They'll have to come out. I'll be putting in yews. Should've been done a hundred years ago. Yews, you can depend on yews. We'll do the planting before it gets cold. Best chance to get well rooted."

"Yes, well . . . Mr. O'Boyle? Were you nearby yesterday? When that man was struck down? It was right *there*"—and Torrey waved a hand toward the brambles.

Sean O'Boyle shook his head. "I only heard about it. I was in the greenhouse, back of the hall. Setting out seedlings. And there's the herbs. Time to shift them around, what with the sun moving. Some have got to catch the sun. But like the rosemary . . ." and he explained about the rosemary.

While he was explaining, Torrey got back on her bike. Why was Mr. O'Boyle carrying on so about majoram and rosemary and sage and so on? She'd only asked a simple question. To which he was giving an interminable nonanswer.

"Well, thanks, Mr. O'Boyle. See you soon." Feet on the pedals, she pushed off.

Alone, he stood holding the tape measure, pulling it out and snapping it back. "None of anybody's business," he said under his breath. He looked about at the trees, the shrubs, the things he loved. He was nobody's business himself, either. Stay away from it. Keep to yourself. He lived with

Caitlin, his widowed oldest sister. Caitlin cared for nothing but the church and her television shows. Made him decent meals. He wasn't the only man in Ireland who hadn't married. For some fellows, there wasn't always the money. Or . . . different reasons. Like himself.

He put the tape measure in his pocket and started back up the avenue, he had plantings to do in the greenhouse. For himself, he was careful, always careful. He kept his fingernails dirty and a bit of stubble on his chin. In O'Malley's, he talked about the soccer scores as though he cared. He drank just the one pint, being cautious. Sipped at it. Times when he was parched for a second pint. But resisted. The one pint make his thighs weak. Two might make his brain weak. Incautious. About *it*. They'd never understand. Nor did he.

Partway up the avenue, he stopped. The hall in this midafternoon light had a softness, the manor's Georgian splendor was blurred, it looked so like the painting of Sylvester Hall on wall of the main staircase and like those early painting of some of the other great houses or castles of Ireland. He laughed suddenly. Natalie! That first day he'd come to work at Sylvester Hall! A grubby little charmer, a little devil, aged eight, she'd made him laugh. He'd caught her starting to eat the red berries off a bramble bush. Someone had told her you'd die if you ate them, she didn't believe it, she wanted to see if it was really true. That Alcock's Academy must have half torn its hair out, taming down that little whirlwind.

Only nineteen when she'd married Andrew Cameron. Dakin, an early-born baby, was a sturdy little chap. Worshipped his father from day one. The boy was a puppy jumping around at his father's knees. He'd almost lost his mind two years ago when his father was killed in the cross fire.

"Sean!" Breda the cook, squat and fat, was bustling up the avenue from the house toward him. She was carrying a casserole. "Rabbit stew! I promised Caitlin. Enough for two meals for the pair of you. Put it in your car. Not on the seat. Set it on the floor, so it won't tip over. And thank her for the raisin biscuits."

Sean took the casserole from Breda. His connection with Sylvester Hall and the family within it gave him a warm, safe feeling. It was like having a uniform with a crest on the pocket. He was part of something. He belonged.

16

Torrey sat propped up against the pillows in bed with Jasper Shaw. The old quilt lay on the floor at the foot of the bed. They had made love twice, then dozed. A blue haze of evening darkened the windowpanes. It was six o'clock, almost two hours since Torrey had returned home from her encounter with Sean O'Boyle.

Jasper had appeared at the cottage shortly before four o'clock carrying a knapsack and wearing his old moss green sweater and dungarees, as though he hadn't arrived in the gleaming gunmetal Jaguar that as usual he'd left parked in Ballynagh on Butler Street. He'd gained at least a half dozen more pounds. "The more of me to love you, my girl." He'd grinned at her, and his nostrils twitched as they always did when he said something he thought was funny. He had a narrow nose in a longish kind of Irish face.

Now, lying with one arm beneath Torrey's head, he said comfortably, "All right, *now* you can tell me. A murderous attack? I heard a bit of something on the RTE. A Canadian?"

"Yes. I was bicycling on the road over the bridge, the road that goes past Sylvester Hall. I almost saw it happen. But not quite, damn it. Tom Brannigan, a man from Montreal. Someone bashed him with a club. Could've broken his head. It was pretty awful. There's a piece in the *Independent* about the attack. It's on the bureau in the kitchen. This Brannigan had arrived in Ballynagh only a couple of hours earlier. He'd put up at Nolans. Likely a tourist, but nobody knows." She shivered, suddenly chilled. "Funny thing, I saw him having a pint in O'Malley's maybe a half hour before he was attacked. Anyway, you can read the piece."

"I will." Jasper yawned. "So . . . peaceful village life gets a bit of a shaking up. Stimulating. Keeps the blood flowing. Right? Unfortunately some of the blood was Mr. Brannigan's. What else have I missed? Besides you, of course." His hand affectionately caressed her nape the way she loved.

"There *is* something else."

"Do tell." Jasper resettled the pillow behind his back.

"Well . . ." She told him then about the threatening telephone call when Dakin was working at the cottage and how after he'd left, she'd gone into the woods. "Look at this." She took the old tin lozenge box from the drawer in the bedside table, opened it, and held up the cigarette butt she'd found under the oak. "I can't tell the brand. There's an *S*, then I think an *I*. The rest's burned away. It's imposs—"

"Sinbad," Jasper said. "Relatively new. Canadian company. Getting popular up there."

"Ca*na*dian?" For a moment she was bewildered. Then she felt a protest rising in her. No, *no*! Head bent, she put the cigarette butt back in the box. Slowly she closed the lid. She didn't want to look at Jasper.

"Say it," Jasper said.

"Well . . . coincidence."

"Coincidence?" Jasper said. "That the man on the telephone threatening Dakin Cameron's mother was likely Canadian . . . at least that Sinbad cigarette butt suggests it. And Brannigan, whom *some*one then bashed at the Sylvester Hall gates—I'm only saying *some*one—tried to kill—was a Canadian? A Canadian who might have made a threatening call to

Dakin Cameron and was a threatening presence to Natalie Cameron? A Canadian who was presumably terrorizing—"

"I don't think—"

"The boy. Dakin. Close to his mother? Maybe, if he were sufficiently spooked—What's he like?"

"*Like*?" She stared at Jasper, but she was seeing the leering faces of the two Dublin lads on the access road as she bicycled toward them, she was seeing the dirty hand that grasped the handlebars, stopping her. She was seeing, then, the blur of a mustard jersey on her left, she was hearing a voice saying to the dirty hand's owner, "You don't really mean that, do you?" and in response to have the other Dublin boy lash at his face and land a blow. And in return get clobbered.

"Like?" she said to Jasper; and she told him about the encounter on the road. "I'd say he's more a knight errant. Not likely to attack anyone except to defend himself."

At seven o'clock they left the cottage and walked up the road to the village. Jasper didn't want to miss Finney's Monday night supper special of stew made with lamb shanks, carrots, curry, and stout, a four-star dish, in his estimation. Next week he'd be at the Kinsale Food Festival savoring and tasting, and reporting on Kinsale's famous restaurants in "Jasper," his food column.

They came into Finneys, to the warmth and the usual suppertime hubbub. At the bar a handful of local farmhands and shop owners were deep into politics and swapping local gossip. One tiddly old fellow, holding on to the bar, was humming "Reilly's Daughter."

Torrey and Jasper settled at the only available table, one of a small cluster of tables beside the bar, and Torrey said hello to Sergeant Bryson and Ms. Plant, who were finishing supper at the next table. Ms. Plant was having wine with her lamb shanks, Jimmy Bryson a dark beer. Torrey smiled at

Jimmy Bryson. Thoughtful of him to take Ms. Plant to supper. Never mind that it was at the Ballynach village expense. Ms. Plant, sipping the last of her wine, had managed to pull her rather fleshy self together. She was in a soft brown wool dress, and with her hair now neatly combed she looked composed and even attractive despite an overabundance of blue eye shadow.

Jasper had just ordered when the tiddly old fellow at the bar said to his younger companion, "That fishing chap, with the suede fishing hat? Fished for a bit of cuddly and caught himself a lulu. Billy spied them going into her studio, O'Sullivan's old barn. Fancy bit of fishing, all right!" He put a finger aside his nose and snickered. "She's not got much of a reputation as a *painter*, but the *other*—"

"Shut up, Danny!" Sergeant Bryson glared at the old fellow. "Shut up! There's ladies around!" And it was true, the shocked look on Ms. Plant's face.

As Torrey said to Jasper five minutes later, after Sergeant Bryson and Ms. Plant had left, "For a second, I thought that the gallant Sergeant Bryson would take a swing at that old fellow." Was it possible, she wondered, that Sergeant James Bryson, aged twenty-four, was a bit too protective of Ms. Brenda Plant, who was certainly at least in her mid forties. Yet there was something about the set of his shoulders, so protective, as Ms. Brenda Plant preceded him out of Finney's.

"Worth ten lines in 'Jasper,' that lamb shanks with curry," Jasper said when two hours later they got back to the cottage. They were barely inside when rain spattered on the windowpanes and gusts of wind rattled the windows. Jasper put more peat on the fire and added a handful of coal.

Torrey settled down on the shabby old couch with the third Georges Simenon. Jealousy, a lawyer husband with a mistress, murder. It all took place in Paris. But in good, colloquial Hungarian. The clock on the dresser ticked. The rain made it feel cozy inside.

"How about this one?" Jasper said. He was lazing at the kitchen table with his tattered *Official Guide*. " 'Abram's advice: When eating an elephant take one bite at a time.' "

"Hmmm?" She ought to read the Hungarian aloud, though, get the rhythm of phrases. A smart *tolmacs* — "interpreter," in Hungarian — would do that.

"Or this one," Jasper said: " 'Jinny's law: There is no such thing as a short beer. As in "I'm going to stop off at Joe's for a short beer before I meet you." ' "

Torrey blinked. Not Joe's for a short beer. O'Malley's. A short beer. Strange that Thomas Brannigan of Montreal had stopped in at O'Malley's for a beer he hadn't even touched. His narrow, pale face had been thundrous with anger, his jaw clenched. She could see him now, standing at the bar, scrutinizing everyone who came in, watching, even, to see who came out of the men's room. And that untouched glass of beer on the bar before him. Then abruptly he was gone.

17

On Tuesday morning a few minutes before noon Natalie Cameron arrived back from an early-morning meeting in Dunlavin where she'd passionately supported a low-cost housing proposal. In the front hall, she picked up the morning's mail from the tray, stared down at the letter, and tore it open. The message this time was on a scrap of ruled paper:

Tuesday noon at the cairn. Forty thousand pounds. If you don't appear, Cloverleaf goes to the Dublin papers. An ugly tale for your son and fiancé to hear on television news or read about in the press. This is final.

The sharp handwriting had dug into the paper.

Natalie cried out, an inarticulate cry of . . . anger? fear? rage? She hardly knew. She crushed the letter spasmodically in a fist.

"Ma'am?" Jessie, coming from the kitchen, looked alarmed. "Is something the matter?"

"No . . . no." She ran past Jessie and up the stairs In her bedroom, she went directly to the dresser, fumbled out what she wanted and ran back down the stairs. Jessie was still in the front hall, looking worried, and said instantly, "Mrs. Cameron? Rose at Castle Moore says Coyle's has raspberries, I can get some for lunch if you—"

"Never mind." She tried to pull herself together, Jessie was looking at her so funny. Lunch seemed a foreign word. "Eggs—eggs will do, Jessie. Omelettes? Dakin's off on a job." Luce was at school. "Eggs. I'll be back in—shortly." In her right-hand jacket pocket her fist tightened on the letter.

Past the coach house, walking fast, she turned left and climbed over the rail fence and half ran across the meadow, the long, dry grass swishing against her pants legs. She'd meet him, all right, this blackmailer! She drew in a breath that turned into a shuddering sob. She reached the stand of fir trees where the woods began and passed the tree where as a child she'd buried treasures of dolls' clothes, bits of gimcrack jewelry, play money.

She walked faster. Her brogues scattered dry leaves. Sun filtered through the trees. In a minute she'd come out at the ridge and reach the cairn, that pile of stones marking the division between Sylvester Hall and Castle Moore.

Cloverleaf? It meant nothing to her.

A thought widened her eyes and slowed her steps. What if . . . Could this extortionist know some secret about Andrew? Something she'd been ignorant of? Loving Andrew, bearing his children, was there something hidden that all along she hadn't suspected? Another life? She thought of Andrew's business trips to Dublin, she saw him walking up a garden path to a secret little house in Ballsbridge, saw a door opening, heard a woman's lilting voice—

Oh, *stop* it! Not Andrew! Never. Besides, the extortionist's first letter had said *a revelation about you,* hadn't it?

For a moment, she faltered. She brushed a hand across her eyes. Something, a flash of light, a glimpse of a yellow party dress, shutter-clicked across her vision and was gone. She slowed, then hurried on. All around her was the peaceful countryside looking like a tourist's brochure of the Irish landscape in Wicklow, the field with the hillocks of green, the tumbled stone fence enclosing it, the mountains beyond, and high on their slopes the scattering of grazing sheep. So innocent.

She slowed again, feeling a growing uncertainty. It was madness to come to meet this blackmailer. He was crazy indeed to expect her to deliver forty thousand pounds on a Tuesday morning. Did he think she kept money in her dresser drawer rather than in a Dublin bank? But no, he must know how in hours she could access it through her money market.

But . . . And now she stopped. It was not the blackmailer's presumed madness but something else, some inner turbulence, a questioning, a fear, something frightening her because of what she had brought with her in her left-hand pocket, while the blackmail note was in her right-hand pocket.

She took a breath. She could see a figure standing under the oak tree by the cairn.

She crossed the field.

18

"Mushrooms!" Sheila said, "Winifred! We could get poisoned. You can't just—"

"Don't be silly. The illustrations are precise. *Mushroom Gathering*, by Dodson Barnaby. Cost me fourteen pounds." Winifred turned pages. "Recipes in the back."

It was Tuesday morning, ten o'clock. They were in the tower room at Castle Moore, it was where Winifred wrote her poetry whenever she stayed at the castle. She used a quill pen for the occasional romantic poem and her state-of-the-art laptop for the others.

"But *Wini*fred! What about that Sacha Guitry film, *The Story of a Cheat*? The whole family of thirteen died after dinner from eating mushrooms they'd picked in the woods."

"Yes, Sheila. The whole family, except the boy who'd been bad and was sent to bed without any dinner. That's a lesson to profit by, as he decided: be bad and stay alive to have a good and naughty time."

"Winifred, really! Sometimes you make me—"

"Sheila, do go down, it's too cold up here for you, you're turning blue. Besides, I want to work on a new villanelle about Irish women. I'm going to make it sound centuries old, the time of ladies weaving tapestries and the like. But I want the reader to slowly realize, with a little frisson, that it's about Irishwomen in the year 2002."

Sheila said, "Rosie is fixing lunch now. Ham sandwiches." And at the door, "At least I know *they* won't kill me."

Winifred, picking up the quill pen, said, "We can go after lunch and my yoga. We'll take the basket Rose uses for the kitchen garden. And the Barnaby."

19

The sun was in Natalie's eyes, it flickered through the trees, so that she saw only the man's figure. She squinted and moved aside. Now she could see his face.

Pale eyes were looking back at her from a flat-cheeked face. It was a sensual face with a jutting mouth that right now bore a triumphant smile. His hair, faintly receding, was brown and looked dyed. He could be in his midforties. He looked fit, as though he worked out. He wore corduroys and an expensive-looking, diamond-patterned sweater. A brimmed suede hat lay on the cairn beside him; it had left a faint red mark on his forehead. "Well, now." He surveyed her. "Finally! Wasted my time. You should've known better."

Not an Irishman. American accent? Australian? A cultivated accent. She stared at him. He wasn't quite the Cro-Magnon man, the brute she had visualized.

"Well? Come on! The money! I haven't time to dither around."

She was too enraged to speak. Her heart was beating hard. When her voice came out, it was hoarse and almost strangled in her throat. "Who are you? I don't know what your letters mean! And those trinkets! I—"

The man's eyes went narrow. He took a step toward her.

There under the trees, she hated his closeness. "You—Where's the money?"

"I don't understand any of it! You've made some kind of mistake. I haven't any past! I haven't any secrets for you to blackmail me about! I came to tell you—"

"The *money*," the man said. His voice was incredulous. "The forty thousand pounds! *You didn't bring the money?*"

"No, it's all wrong!" She was shaking. In the right-hand pocket of her jacket, her fist closed spasmodically on his third note. "I don't know, for instance, what you mean by Cloverleaf."

"Liar," the man said softly. "If you know anything you know Cloverleaf. The last thing you'd have wanted to know."

She was in a nightmare. Was she really under the trees by the cairn at this corner of the Sylvester Hall lands? A nightmare, but here she was, sun filtering through the trees. The worst of the nightmare was that it bore some dreadful kind of reality just outside her reach.

"You . . ." The man's face was furious. He reached out and gripped her arm. "You—"

"No!" She wrenched her arm free. "No! *You!* Invading Sylvester Hall! Sneaking in and creeping up the stairs and stealing my father's, my—" For now *she* was the furious one, frightened but furious, and she dug her hand into her left-hand pocket and pulled out her father's ivory penknife. Her hand shook as she held it out for him to see. "You stole it! My father's, my—"

The man stared at her holding the penknife. He said roughly, "Are you crazy?" He reached out and snatched the penknife from her hand. He was looking at her so strangely that her confusing, bewildering fear made her tremble. Then the man shook his head as though to clear it. He stepped away.

A breeze had sprung up, leaves scattered down from the

69

trees, turning in the sunlight. What now, Natalie thought, what now? But she was immediately to know, for the extortionist stepped close to her, his flat-cheeked face fierce in its anger. "You lying bitch! Enough of your games! I want forty thousand pounds *now*! Or—" He raised the penknife in a menacing gesture. "Or I will cut your life to pieces! They will know about Dakin. And what you are." His narrow, pale eyes glared at her. "You have an hour." He stepped away. "I haven't much time. A bank check will have to do. After I cash it, I will send you the Cloverleaf." He gave a short laugh. "You'll have to trust me."

From the cluster of trees, he watched her flee, blundering and tripping across the field. Liar that she was! He hadn't even had a chance to lay out the brutal facts, to spit out what he knew. He frowned, thinking of what she'd said about him stealing the penknife from Sylvester Hall. Because of course he hadn't stolen it. She knew that very well! Was she deviously clever? Apparently. For all the good it would do her!

Damn her! The money. He looked at his watch. An hour. After that, if she didn't come, he would show no mercy.

He picked up his suede hat, slapped it against his leg, and leaned back against the oak.

20

At Glasshill Hospital, Inspector O'Hare looked bitterly down at the unconscious man in the high, white bed. A bulky bandage slanted across his temple and was wound around his head; his face bore blue bruises; his eyes were closed, the lids a faint lavender. His lips were so pale they looked bloodless. Unconscious, blast it! Informative as a piece of wood. What a cock-up!

"I'm sorry, Inspector," Head Nurse Huddleson, a buxom woman in her fifties, said apologetically at his elbow. "Mr. Brannigan became conscious. And the way he was talking, agitated, garbled, and so frightening, what with every other word being 'kill.' So when I called and spoke to your Sergeant Bryson on the phone—"

"Yes, I see." O'Hare wanted to lean down and shake the unconscious man awake. The trip from Ballynagh to Glasshill, thirty miles away, had been a time waster. The Tuesday traffic, ordinarily light, had been stalled because of an accident. If he'd used the police car instead of his Honda, he could've sirened his way through, blast it! Sergeant Bryson was still too much a novice to be sent to interview the injured man. So he'd had no choice.

"I only *thought*," Nurse Huddleson began, but stopped short at a moan from the bandaged man. Brannigan's eyes

71

were closed, but the lids were twitching. Two deep lines formed between his brows. He jerked his head from side to side, his lips moved and he began to mutter.

"There, you see!" Nurse Huddleson was triumphant.

O'Hare slipped his notebook from his pocket and found his pen. The mutter was turning into words, at first indistinguishable, then clearly, "The old woman lied to me! Trapped, penniless . . . There were keys in a green marble ashtray on the dashboard. 'You push the button to make it open.' "

Brannigan moved his head more violently from side to side. Suddenly he cried out, arched his back, and raised up, throwing his head back. *"It was a thunderclap!"* A heave, and he was half out of the bed, arms flailing, eyes open and staring.

"Aldrich!" Nurse Huddleson grasped at the flailing arms, *"Nurse Aldrich! Dr. Conners!"* O'Hare lunged forward and heaved Brannigan's body back onto the bed, and heard behind him a "Christ!" and swift footsteps; a white-coated arm reached past, held up a hypodermic, and plunged it into Tom Brannigan's upper arm. Brannigan's arched body collapsed, his staring eyes closed. He breathed evenly.

"Well, now." O'Hare straightened his police jacket and picked up his notebook from the floor.

Dr Conners, a young man with tired eyes, accompanied him out through the main hall. "It'll be at least a week, maybe longer," Conners said, "before we'll see the light of day. Mr. Brannigan sustained a blow of considerable force. A heavy stick, was it, Inspector?"

"So we believe. But nothing found. As yet."

21

In the coach house, gasping for breath, Natalie pulled the door to the carriage closed and sank back against the faded upholstery. She'd fled so crazily from the blackmailer that her heart was pounding. Quiet down, quiet *down*!

She drew a deep breath. He had to be a madman. She gave a shaky laugh. Belatedly, she'd get help. A fog had somehow slid across her vision bringing hallucinations, a residue probably of the dreadful loss of Andrew. The only reality was the man waiting at the cairn. A man who had stolen a penknife.

Her heart was no longer pounding but beginning to beat regularly. She breathed in the musty, comforting smell of the old carriage. She'd rest here for a few minutes. Then she'd call Inspector O'Hare. She'd make some excuse for not having come to him earlier when she'd received that first threatening letter. No matter. There had been three letters. There'd be a fourth. He wouldn't give up. The Gardai would stake out the cairn.

Later, Marshall, back from the States, would lovingly reproach her with, "But why didn't you call me at once?" and he'd hug her close. By next month she'd be dining out on her blackmail tale.

In the carriage, she glanced at her watch. Right now, she'd find Dakin and tell him that she was going to Inspector O'Hare for help after all. Dakin was so angry at the threat to her, so ready to do battle on her account, that it had worried her.

She'd rest a minute here in the carriage before looking for Dakin. She ran a finger along the armrest; the figured mulberry velvet was now so worn, so old and faded. You could barely distinguish the entwined flowers, the shapes of reclining hounds. When had the carriage started to become her refuge? So many years ago, yes, even before Andrew was killed. She'd settle snugly into this old carriage in the corner of the coach house with a feeling of being loved. Sometimes she'd drowse and wake to find herself smiling, warm, hearing whispers, rubbing a cheek against the mulberry velvet . . . no, not the mulberry. The fabric was something else, it was twill, she could feel the tiny ridges of the twill, she smelled the masculine smell that came from it, she could even see the color of the twill, it was dark blue. . . .

On the worn mulberry velvet her hand went still. Her eyes opened wide. Minutes passed. Then, mouth dry, she whispered: "Cloverleaf."

She was running now, running fast back toward the cairn. An hour! *Hurry!* She must get to him in time, tell him she'd have the money for him right away! She'd get it from her brokerage account. But she'd left him almost an hour ago! If he wasn't still at the cairn, she'd run to Ballynach, search everywhere, he could be in Finney's Restaurant or in O'Malley's, he could be staying at Nolan's Bed and Breakfast, or . . . where? *Where?* Suppose, vindictive, he was already calling RTV and the press. A sob caught in her throat.

Through the meadow grass, panting, past the fir with her childhood buried treasure she ran, a pain in her chest. *Cloverleaf, an ugly tale for your son to hear.* Legs trembling, she was stumbling now, hurry, *hurry!* She was crossing the field toward the big oak by the cairn, praying he was still there, praying to see the hateful pale eyes and the jutting mouth, and not daring even to take an instant to glance at her watch. The pain sharp in her chest, she reached the oak that shadowed the cairn.

22

"Mushrooms like damp places," Winifred said to Sheila, who lagged unhappily behind with the basket from the kitchen garden. They had left Castle Moore a half hour earlier. "After a rain, mushrooms just spring up. Particularly at the base of oaks."

Winifred strode cheerfully ahead, the Barnaby book under her arm. Crushed down on her head was an old Girl Guide hat with the brim pinned up on one side. She wore her favorite flannel shirt, knickers, and hiking boots. Sheila, in a heavy woolen skirt and sweater, longed for an after-lunch nap. Nettles clung to her skirt and she was cold. The basket she carried was padded with a soft dishtowel to hold the gathered mushrooms. So far it was empty. To Sheila's relief, Winifred's careful scrutiny of the sides of rotting logs and bases of trees had turned up not a single mushroom.

"I *still* think," Sheila said, "that we're taking our life in—"

"I'm not a mycologist, Sheila, but"—and Winifred held up the book—"Barnaby says there are three thousand and three hundred species of mushrooms in the world and—"

"I *know*, you *told* me! More than two thousand are harmless. But which are which? It only takes maybe one tiny little poisonous mushroom, one single innocent-looking—"

"And we'll keel over with our claws in the air? I'm going by the illustrations, Sheila. Barnaby has *red* dots on poisonous mushrooms like destroying angel, *Amanita virosa*, and death cap, *Amanita phalloides*. We'll pick only Barnaby's *blue* dot mushrooms. The edible ones. Like the wood mushroom. *Agaricus silvicola. Silvicola* means 'living in woods,' Sheila."

"But—"

"And the horse mushroom. Edible. *Agaricus arvensis. Arvensis* means 'growing in fields.' But we'll be careful there because Barnaby warns that it can be confused with destroying angel. But destroying angel has pure white gills and a saclike volva at the base of the stem. So, no problem."

Sheila made a whimpering sound.

In ten minutes they reached the bridle path belonging to Castle Moore. "There are ancient oaks, beyond," Winifred said, "and plenty of forest, we'll have good luck." They crossed the bridle path and pushed on through thick gorse. A fallen log looked promising. Winifred knelt and studied the whitish growth minutely, referring to the Barnaby. "Lichen," she decided. Sheila gave a shudder of relief. They went on. A hundred yards farther was a meadow, beyond which was forest. Winifred squinted across the meadow to a ridge of oaks. "Beautiful and ancient. Probably were here at the time of the Druids. If you believe in that sort of thing. Personally, I do. That big one marks the dividing line between Castle Moore and Sylvester Hall. Shady under those oaks, and certainly damp after last night's rain. Stop *lagging*, Sheila."

They crossed the meadow and came under the shade of the big oak beside the cairn. There were only flecks of sunlight coming through the leaves, flecks that were like a scattering of gold coins, the scattering of gold flickering down on the figure of Natalie Cameron, who stood holding what looked like a small knife.

A man's blood-soaked body lay at her feet.

23

It brought to O'Hare's mind a sacrifice he'd once seen as a kid in a frightening biblical illustration, the goat's throat slit, blood soaking into the desert sand, a line of camels in the distance, though of course this was Gaelic country, autumn leaves, birds chirping, a fresh breeze.

O'Hare made a repudiating, whistling sound between his teeth. The man's body lay faceup beside the cairn. Blood from his gaping, slit throat had soaked his diamond-patterned sweater and clotted the leaves around him. Bloodless, dead white face. He was no one O'Hare had ever seen before.

O'Hare swallowed with difficulty and looked about. Natalie Cameron stood a few feet away, head hanging, eyes dazed, hair in a tangle. Sergeant Bryson was relieving her of the penknife gently, adroitly, with his hand in a plastic sandwich bag so as not to smudge the prints. Dreadful, unbelievable. Yet incontrovertible.

Winifred Moore was standing at his left, and beyond her was Sheila Flaxton. Winifred was smoking one of her brown cigarettes, a book under her arm. She had called him ten minutes ago on the cell phone that was always on her belt. She'd said enough for him to avoid wasting time: he'd phoned headquarters of the Garda Síochána, the Irish police, at Dublin

Castle, Phoenix Park; the van with the technical staff would be arriving in thirty or forty minutes. The Dublin Metropolitan area comprised Dublin city and the greater part of the county and portions of County Kildare and Wicklow.

"I'm going to be *sick*," Sheila Flaxton said.

"No need to stay." O'Hare was jotting down notes. "Nor you, Ms. Moore. We'll be in touch."

"Hmmm?" Winifred Moore said. She was looking off across the meadow. She grinned. "No surprise."

Inspector O'Hare followed her gaze. Crossing the meadow toward them, walking swiftly, was Ms. Torrey Tunet.

"So," Torrey said to Jasper, slathering butter on the brown bread that Jasper had baked and taken from the oven a half hour earlier, "when I got to Sylvester Hall, and Jessie told me that just ten minutes before, Natalie Cameron'd come tearing out of the coach house hysterically saying, "The cairn, the cairn!' and I'd only come to the hall to ask her about trying some late plantings of—"

" 'Only to ask her' nothing," Jasper said. "Late plantings! *You?* Hah!" They were at the kitchen table, it was four o'clock, and a fire in the hearth warmed the kitchen. Jasper grinned at Torrey and refilled her teacup. "Your color's high, rose on a peach; you look as made-up as Gilbert and Sullivan's ladies in *The Mikado.* Insupportable excitement. You can't keep your nose out—"

"That's got nothing to do with it. I'm—"

"Looking for trouble. You don't believe Natalie Cameron managed to slit that fellow's throat with a penknife, right? Hardly possible, either. A penknife! And Natalie Cameron could never have committed such a horrible crime, right? After all, she's your friend Dakin's mother and you've met her for all of ten minutes. So, in your considered—"

"Stick to your shortnin' bread," Torrey said. "Besides, I'm not going to *do* anything." She took a sip of tea.

At six o'clock, Inspector O'Hare telephoned his wife, Noreen. He'd be an hour late for supper. There'd been phone calls and faxes to and from Chief Superintendent O'Reilley at Dublin Castle. Sergeant Bryson had typed up the report. Meantime, the murder, already known as the Cairn murder was on the six o'clock RTE news.

Natalie Sylvester Cameron, thirty-six, of Sylvester Hall, Ballynagh, Wicklow, arrested in connection with the murder of Raphael Ricard, forty-four, of Montreal, Canada. According to Inspector Egan O'Hare of Ballynagh, Mr. Ricard, a financial advisor on a fishing vacation, was killed with a small penknife, his throat slit. No known motive as yet. Mrs. Cameron is at Sylvester Hall, bail having been furnished by her attorney, Daniel Morton.

O'Hare rubbed his eyes, then doled out a large-sized dog biscuit to Nelson, who ambled over to his blanket by the soda machine and settled down with the biscuit.

"I just *gave* him a biscuit," Sergeant Bryson said from over at the computer.

"Then he's a lucky dog," O'Hare said. He tapped the desk with his fingertips, frowning. The penknife was already in the forensic department at Dublin Castle in Phoenix Park. But what motive? What was the Canadian to Natalie Cameron that she'd killed him?

An hour ago, Natalie Cameron had sat right here beside his desk. Her bloodied sweater and shirt were in a plastic bag on the shelf, already tagged for Dublin Castle. Natalie Cameron wore an old plaid jacket of Jimmy Bryson's that had hung on a hook by the police station door for months. She was waiting for her attorney from Dublin; he would make bail. In a husky whisper she told the horror of it, hazel eyes wide with shock. "Yes, Inspector, I was out walking. I came to the cairn and saw him lying there, blood thick around—It was horrible! I thought, 'Go for help!' But then. . . . I could tell he was dead. I picked up the knife without thinking . . . What, Inspector? No, a man I never saw before." And "The knife? I recognized it. My father's penknife . . . No I don't know how it came to be there. . . . Objects have been stolen from Sylvester Hall before, the doors are always left open for the dogs to go in and out. . . . Yes, Inspector, I picked it up, I suppose I was in shock. The man's appalling-looking body, after all! One hardly expects . . ."

After she was gone, accompanied by her attorney, Sergeant Bryson swung around in his chair by the fax machine. "Out for a walk, was she? Far's I know from Jessie, going out for a walk Mrs. Cameron'd always whistle for the dogs to come. That was her habit. But this time she'd gone off alone."

Inspector O'Hare gave Jimmy Bryson a surprised look. More to the lad than he'd thought.

"Another thing," Sergeant Bryson said, "What about them both being Canadians—this murdered fellow, Ricard, and the other one, Brannigan, who was attacked at the Sylvester Hall gates? What's the connection?"

O'Hare rubbed his eyes. So far, their only information about Raphael Ricard came from his passport, driver's license, and business cards, all of which had been among his effects at Nolan's Bed and Breakfast. "We'll have the Montreal police report on Ricard by tomorrow, Jimmy." Maybe the report would reveal not only a connection to Brannigan but to Natalie Cameron.

24

At nine-thirty Wednesday morning, Torrey braked her bike to a stop at the entrance to Sylvester Hall. Two furiously barking hounds came running from the mansion.

"Crackers! Buster!" Jessie, in the doorway in her aproned uniform, clapped her hands and the dogs turned and raced inside. "They're fake fierce, Ms. Tunet," Jessie said. "They're really cream puffs."

"I would've called," Torrey said, "but my phone's out." The lie came easily. "I wondered—even with all the tragic—the unfortunate events, I came because I'm hoping Dakin can do some more work for me at the cottage." Another lie.

"Dakin's gone off, he didn't say where. Ms. Cameron's left for Dublin to meet with her attorney. We're all so upset! There've been reporters and photographers, come like a swarm of bees all yesterday afternoon. But we stayed closed up, even the shutters."

Jackpot! Nobody home. "I can imagine!" Torrey shivered. "Frightening, what's happened. And now, so dismal! Such a damp and chilly morning! More like November. I should've worn something heavier." *Take pity on the poor little match girl that I am!*

"Well . . . if you don't mind the kitchen, Ms. Tunet, Breda's made a full pot and there's brown bread."

"So," Jessie said, elbows on the long kitchen table, teacup in both hands, "back then, in Sybil Sylvester's time, my mam was housekeeper. Those days! Sybil Sylvester oversaw the land and stock with an eye like a magnifying glass. As for the household! My mam, in charge of the household, had to count the linens, see to their repair, no raveled edges, no rips or tears. Then there was the china, the silver, the maids and cleaning. It was 'Mrs. Dugan this, Mrs. Dugan that.' My mam was run ragged."

"My!" Torrey spooned sugar into her tea.

"Ms. Sybil checked every day how much Moira the cook spent and where she traded. Every *day*, my mam said. And the gardens! Checking right down to the seeds Sean O'Boyle put in the ground and the plants he was growing in the hothouse."

"My!" Torrey sipped.

"Same thing with the young one, Natalie. Her marks at school, from the time she was left in Ms. Sybil's care. What she was allowed to eat. The weekly laundering of the white school blouses and maroon ties and knee socks she wore to that school. Along with the cleaning of the navy blazer and pleated skirt. Disciplinarian sort of place, Alcock's Academy. Strict. Kept the girls close. And studying hard. There was only that one time when Natalie and another little girl, her best friend, were caught smoking. They were about fourteen, then. Quite a fuss Ms. Sybil made. Blamed the school. Then, let's see. There was the chauffeur, Olin Caughey with the red nose, who took care of the cars, that silver Rolls, and some other car, I don't remember. Had to account for every drop of petrol, or she'd have had his head on a platter."

Breda, the cook, fifty, dumpy, and hard breathing, shook her head in admiration. "I wasn't here then, but I've heard. A proper overseer, Sybil Sylvester!"

"Well," Jessie said, "except for the time she had the burst

appendix. Had to be rushed to the hospital. Weeks it was. My mam said it was the only time, with Ms. Sybil out of the way, *she'd* had a chance to relax!"

"The appendix," Torrey said. "When would that've been?"

"Ummm . . . fifteen, twenty years ago. My mam said it was touch and go. Ms. Sybil had to stay in bed almost a month. August, it was. Then, after, for a while, she'd only go out for a half hour's drive of an afternoon."

The kitchen clock struck nine, Jessie got up. "More tea, if you'd like, Ms. Tunet, and try one of the buns. Breda will keep you company, I've to do the bedrooms and the marketing. You've got the list, Breda?"

Torrey got up. "Thanks, Jessie. I'm going." She went toward the door, then turned. "Jessie? That other little girl, Natalie's friend? Who was she?"

"Ho! Came of a proper family, that one! Not that you'd know it now! She's still about. Paints pictures in O'Sullivan's barn. Wild parties and such. Divorced more than once. Back to using her own name. Kate Burnside."

25

Ma?" In the far, dusty corner of the coach house, Dakin turned the tarnished gilt latch and pulled open the carriage door. But the carriage was empty. Odd, he could smell her perfume; she had to be about. "Your mother? She came back from Dublin an hour ago," Jessie had told him ten minutes ago when he'd got home. Yet he couldn't find her, she wasn't in her bedroom or the library or anywhere in the house.

"Ma?"

"Over here." Click of a car door opening. He turned around. The old silver Rolls. He was surprised. It had never been the Rolls, always the carriage. His mother stepped out of the car. Dakin, approaching, felt a wave of compassion. His mother's beautiful eyes under the black brows were haggard; she had pushed her hair behind her ears, but wisps fell untidily across her cheeks. The skirted gray suit she'd worn to Dublin was rumpled and there was a stain—wine?—on one lapel; lunch with the attorney and his legal associate must have been a misery. His mother! Always so forthright, so warmhearted and funny. And now involved in this nightmare.

"What, darling?" She was looking at him, looking so closely that he felt a tightening behind his ears, a wariness. Not that she could know, or suspect; it had been his secret for two years.

"Ma! I've been looking all — When will Marshall get here? He'll know what to do. What did he say? How long before he gets here? By tonight?"

She didn't answer. She was still looking at him in that strange way. As though she had never seen him before. Studying him. It gave him a bereft feeling, like being in a boat that had lost its mooring.

"Ma? *When?*" Marshall was a master at handling difficult situations, getting to the nub. In his wars for decent housing, he'd learned brilliant legal ways to scatter enemy troops. That was all that was necessary. In this case; get them off the scent. *Get them off the scent!* "Ma?"

His mother said wearily, "I didn't call Marshall." She was twisting the ring on her finger, the diamond engagement ring that Marshall West had slipped on her finger barely two weeks earlier. "I'm not going to."

"You . . . What do you — *Why?*"

"Because I'm not, Dakin, that's all. I'm not."

26

Dry leaves crunched under Torrey's brogues as she approached the O'Sullivan's barn.

Snoop. From the Dutch. Irresistible. Like being a buckskin-clad Indian in a forest scenting something in the wind, following a trail, seeing the vestige of a hoofprint on a leaf, a bit of earth freshly turned up, seeing overhead the lazy wheeling of a hawk that would make a sudden plunge.

How had Jessie put it? *Back then, the two fourteen-year-old girls caught smoking.* "*Natalie Cameron's best friend.*"

There was no doorbell, no knocker. Just the fifteen-foot-high barn doors and a shiny black lock. Torrey glanced up. Above, a bank of small-paned windows.

"Hello?" She knocked, then waited, looking about. The O'Sullivan's farmhouse in the distance was unoccupied, there was only this rented barn; it lay in a field that was mostly furze, the spiny shrubs with their yellow flowers now turned brown and dry. A rutted road led to the barn; a blue convertible BMW, dried spatters of mud on its sides, stood a few feet from the barn door.

Torrey called again, louder, "Hell*o!*"

"Give it a push!"

Torrey pushed open the barn door and came into an enormous room, paintings leaning against the walls. She was aware of an unmade bed with a tumble of silken blankets sliding off it, she smelled whisky and perfume, she saw a refrigerator door ajar, but mostly she saw Kate Burnside, who stood in front of a mirror in a plum-colored robe that hung open, revealing nakedness. She was apparently having difficulty trying to comb her long, black hair. At that moment, the comb hit a snarl and slipped from her hand. "*Shit!*" She kicked the comb aside and looked at Torrey. Her eyes were bloodshot, her face a little swollen. "Oh . . . I thought you were Nora. My sometime maid. You're what's-your-name. From Castle Moore's old groundsman's cottage." She pulled her robe closed and tied the sash.

"Yes, Torrey Tunet."

Kate Burnside had to be approaching forty. She was still a beauty, though the ravages of late nights and unchecked drinking had drawn lines around her lush, pretty mouth. Right now she appeared hung over, shaky, and spooked about something.

Torrey hesitated. It seemed crass, now, to have come here to poke into Kate Burnside's past friendship with Natalie Cameron, considering that Natalie was being charged now with yesterday's gruesome murder. Crass, to snoop into—

"I always have a drink about now. What about you?" Kate Burnside wiggled her bare feet into floppy slippers and padded to a sideboard. She picked up a bottle.

"Too early for me," Torrey said. She watched Kate Burnside pour herself a gin. Her hand was shaky. The bottle clinked against the glass.

"Dreadful about Natalie Cameron," Torrey said, "being charged with such a crime! I'm so sorry. I'd only met her once. Jessie at Sylvester Hall was telling me this morning that you and Natalie Cameron were best friends in childhood. Back at Alcock's Academy? And later, in your teens. So I thought—"

Crash! The glass slipped from Kate Burnside's hand and shattered on the floor. She gave a strangled sob and went down on her knees. With her bare hand she began to flick the shards of glass into a pile.

"*Don't!*" Torrey said, too late.

In the bathroom, Torrey put Band-aids on the half dozen cuts on Kate Burnside's fingers. The bathroom was elegant, with a granite tub and an oval-shaped enclosed shower. Really an enviable bathroom, so unlike the makeshift bathroom at the cottage. Here, beside the gleaming shower, was a row of Lucite hooks. And there, on one of the hooks, was a familiar-looking mustard-colored jersey. This one bore the head of a gazelle.

Alone in the barn, sunk back among the pillows on the divan and holding her second gin in her bandaged hand, Kate said aloud, "What *good?*" What good to have told Torrey Tunet anything? What secret she could tell would only bury Natalie deeper. Natalie's great-aunt Sybil, that sweet-faced old bitch, had had influence. Sybil knew people in high places who could, and would, with a quiet phone call here or there, erase things as though they'd never happened. But she, Kate, knew the truth.

She looked down at the gin in her glass. She was seeing Rafe Ricard's disbelieving face, his jutting jaw, when at their first meeting she'd told him why Natalie would never come to the cairn.

"More likely, she'll alert the Gardai," she'd warned him, "They'll trap you!" Lying there in the field, her back protected by his diamond-patterned sweater, she'd been confident he'd give up.

But two days later, this time in O'Sullivan's barn, he'd told her he sent Natalie a third letter. She knew then that she was helpless to make him believe what she had told him about Natalie.

"You don't believe me!" she'd cried out in despair. "But it's true! It's true!" She was wearing her robe and under it a thin silk chemise.

"Liar!" he'd said, half laughing, and he slid a hand through the opening of her robe and caressed the round of her breast, his thumb running back and forth over her nipple, and at his touch she'd felt a swelling and that familiar ache, she couldn't help it. "Liar!" he'd repeated, and he laughed. "You're just trying to protect your friend! Or someone's been having you on! She'll come, all right! She'll come to the cairn on Tuesday with the money and a shivering down to her toes that the truth might out. Pour us a scotch." And he'd loosened his belt.

Now, alone on the divan with her bandaged hand, she couldn't think how insane she must have been to have gone, as in a trance, yet hearing the village clock strike noon that Tuesday—how insane to go to the cairn where Rafe waited for Natalie to show up in response to that third letter. She saw herself crossing the field, her thoughts all mixed up with owing Natalie; it was about Dakin, it was shameful, she'd been shameless. And why was she crossing the field to the cairn? What had she expected to . . . to do? How had she expected to make up for the past?

On the divan, she looked down at her bandaged hand. Blood had seeped through the bandage. She closed her eyes. But she still could see it. Blood was everywhere. On the leaves scattered under the oak. On his jutting jaw. On the diamond-patterned sweater. Blood everywhere.

27

At four-thirty Wednesday afternoon, the door to the police station opened and Sergeant Bryson came in carrying something.

O'Hare stared. "What's that?"

The three-legged stool that Sergeant Jimmy Bryson now carefully set down just inside the door beside Nelson's blanket looked like a dirty old milking stool.

"An antique." Bryson brushed his blue sleeve across the top of the stool, clearing away a bit of dust. "Cost me six pounds. Ms. Plant said I was lucky to've spotted it. It was at the back, behind a coal scuttle, she didn't even see it herself." He stood back and with hands on hips surveyed his purchase. "Lucky I had my day off. We'd gone to five places before—"

"Six *pounds*?"

"Ms. Plant says that in two or three years that stool will fetch double that amount. Triple, even. Say twenty pounds. The longer I hang on, Ms. Plant says, the more valuable it'll be. There's a lot going on about Irish antiques. 'A burgeoning interest,' Ms. Plant says. And not just in America, Ms. Plant says. She says—"

"Sergeant Bryson! We've had a murder in Ballynagh! A gruesome, bloody murder. We've also had an attempted murder, so that a man now lies unconscious in Glasshill Hospital. Antiques!" O'Hare was exasperated. Jimmy Bryson, Sergeant Jimmy Bryson, had been in the garda four years now, he'd hardly begun to shave when he'd started. Eager, interested, promising. And now what? Was he falling prey to a siren's song? A middle-aged siren? Almost as old as his mother. After Ms. Plant's frightening experience at the gates of Sylvester Hall, it was fine that Jimmy, with his soft heart, had offered to take her to Finney's for supper. At the village's expense, of course. Jimmy was a kind young fellow, everybody knew that, and Ms. Plant was alone, and what with her being a bit frightened and upset—But then, Finney's again on Monday night! The lamb shanks, Monday's special. And at Bryson's own expense. And wasn't he using something on his hair? O'Hare could smell it. Even the whites of Sergeant Bryson's eyes looked whiter and his color was high. Not good. And what about young Hannah, up at Castle Moore? Tomorrow was Thursday. Thursday night was Hannah's night off, when Jimmy always took her to the movie at Dunlavin. What about that?

"Going to give it a bit of a wash." Sergeant Bryson picked up the milking stool. Whistling, he carried it across to the bathroom.

Inspector O'Hare looked down at the papers on his desk and at once forgot about Sergeant Jimmy Bryson.

There were two reports. Both concerned Raphael Ricard. The one that had arrived this morning at ten o'clock was from the Montreal Police Department. It gave Raphael Ricard's address, age, marital status (single) and occupation. Three tickets for speeding. Nothing else on the police record.

The second report had arrived an hour ago. It was from Frank Lash, the Dublin attorney representing Natalie Cameron. It had been furnished to Lash by a private detective agency in Montreal. O'Hare reread it for the fifth time.

Raphael Ricard, a financial advisor who pretends to be a cousin of Patrick Ricard, CEO of Pernod Ricard, the world's fifth largest wines and spirit companies with more than eighty brands in forty-five countries of the world . . . a fact that Raphael Ricard is prone to mention in casual conversation.

In actuality Raphael Ricard is the only son of a Quebec grocer and his wife who retired to Florida six years ago. He uses his fictitious ploy of "cousinship" to the CEO who lives in France, to open doors socially in Montreal and obtain accounts as financial advisor to the aspiring newly rich. Cultivates possible clients at social gatherings and at expensive health and exercise clubs. Personal appraisal: risk-taker. Gambler personality. No scruples re women or money. A user.

O'Hare sat back. Raphael Ricard hadn't come to Ballynagh to fish. But what had he to do with Natalie Cameron? Whatever it was, a pity. Tangled butter-colored hair, raising her eyes, trancelike, to Sergeant Bryson when he took the penknife from her. Almost as though she weren't conscious of him or Winifred Moore or any of them around her, or even of the man's body lying almost at her feet.

"Wouldn't be surprised," Sergeant Bryson said, coming from the bathroom with the three-legged stool, "if we've got some antique stuff in the shed at home. Things from my granny and the old man. Could be worth something. When you think of it, half the furniture in every cottage in Ballynagh is antique."

28

Sean O'Boyle started walking down the avenue from Sylvester Hall. Ms. Cameron's check for McGarrey's Nursery was in his pocket. It was getting on to late afternoon, just past four o'clock. McGarrey had promised delivery of the new shrubs at four o'clock. He'd unload the truck at the gates. Sean had his retractable tape measure. He'd set the shrubs along the iron fence, spacing them right. Twenty-four inches apart, say.

He walked briskly for pure enjoyment, breathing deeply of what might be the last of the autumn days scented with apple and hay. He was pleased that he still moved with the gait of a young man. And he had a young figure, too! Never mind his age. He'd have dyed his hair—colored it, they called it now—but in O'Malley's they'd have looked at him sideways, their eyes getting small and suspicious with odd notions, so better not. Besides, what would his sister Caitlin make of it? She was up on everything, what with all she saw on television.

"Mr. O'Boyle! Hel*lo!*"

Ms. Tunet's bike skidded to a stop in front of him. Her short, shiny brown hair, was tossed about by the breeze. Those jeans weren't warm enough, even with this sun, but that was her business. And no jumper on over her jersey. She had a blue knitted muffler around her neck and one end hung down long enough to get tangled in the spokes of her bike. In the bicycle basket was an Irish oatmeal-colored jumper and atop it was a broken-off half of a chocolate bar, the kind with almonds. Ms. Tunet always made him think of the word *lass*, though you didn't hear it much anymore. Except maybe in fake tourist places, putting on the Irish.

"They're all out," Sean said. He'd save her time, she could turn around and go.

"*Act*ually," Ms. Tunet began. Then stopped. She smiled at him and turned her bike around. They walked together toward the gates.

Walking beside Ms. Tunet, Sean was edgy at first. He was sure Ms. Tunet, like everybody else in Ballynagh, would be all excited about Natalie Cameron and the murder. She'd try to pump him about the latest. He couldn't go twenty steps in Ballynagh without someone stopping him with a million questions.

So it was a relief that Ms. Tunet didn't ask him a single thing about the murder. He relaxed and told her about the new shrubs that McGarrey was coming to deliver. She seemed very interested. Maybe she was only being polite, but anyway he went on to explain the different kinds of shrubs to her and why some would thrive along the roadway and others wouldn't. It made conversation that was safe from other things, it was a guard against them.

"You're putting in the same kind of shrubs that were there in Ms. Sybil's day?" Ms. Tunet asked him.

"Yes, the same, they're what Ms. Sybil would've wanted. Ms. Sybil always knew exactly what she wanted. When she told you, it was like it was being handed down from — Excuse me, ma'am, I don't mean —"

"That's all right, Mr. O'Boyle. From what I've heard about

back then, I guess Ms. Sybil was something of a martinet."
And Ms. Tunet laughed.

"Ms. Sybil? Like a martinet?" He snapped and unsnapped
the button on the tape measure in his pocket. "I suppose so."

"Like—well, chatting about the old days, Jessie—or
maybe it was Breda—"

"Breda wasn't *at* Sylvester Hall in the old days. Breda's
been here only six years, so—"

"Well, then, Jessie, I guess. Talking about the price of
petrol, something like that. How the chauffeur back then—"

"Olin Caughey? He was the chauffeur. Half the time in
shirtsleeves, polishing the in*side* of that silver Rolls just the
way Ms. Sybil wanted."

"Well," Ms. Tunet said, "It wasn't about polishing, more
about, well . . . I don't remember. Where's Olin Caughey
now? There's no chauffeur at Sylvester Hall."

Sean gazed down the avenue toward the gates. But he
was seeing Olin Caughey in his blue twill chauffeur's uniform and the black-billed cap on his gray head standing
stiffly by the open door of the Rolls waiting for Ms. Sybil to
come down the steps to go off to one of her bridge games or
dinner parties. "Olin's long gone, Ms. Tunet. Poor old Olin!
Times when he had a tongue as cutting as a buzz saw, but
that was the drink. And when he had the pains. Kidneys a
pest. In hospital that last time, he said to me, 'I'll be like
twenty again.' 'You mean like sixty,' I said back. 'Have to go
on furlough'— that's the way he put it, going into hospital.
'Not out to pasture, mind you,' he told me. 'They'll fix me
up. I'll be back at Sylvester Hall in no time.' He was wrong.
Lived a good six years after, chipper as a squirrel. But never
able to put on his chauffeur's cap again." Sean, remembering, felt sad. In his pocket the tape button went snap, snap.

"His chauffeur's cap?" Ms. Tunet said. "You mean Ms.
Sybil had to hire another chauffeur?"

Sean shook his head. "No, not Ms. Sybil. She was in hospital herself with her appendix when Caughey got that last attack. Caughey got his nephew, his sister's youngest, to come from out around Sligo. By the time Ms. Sybil got home to Sylvester Hall, the young fellow was driving the Rolls smooth as a swan gliding on a pond. *Smoooth* as a swan."

Rumble of McGarrey's Nursery truck. Half past four exactly, and here he and Ms. Tunet were now, at the gates. He gave McGarrey a mock salute.

"What was his name?" Ms. Tunet said. "Olin Caughey's nephew."

"Hmmm? Don't rightly remember. Was only at the hall maybe three, four months. Lived above the coach house, never went into the village. Writing stuff, up there." He was watching the truck. "Jack McGarrey's got a clock for a heart, Ms. Tunet. What about that!" And then, with relief, he was guiding McGarrey's truck, signaling to back the truck to the verge. Ms. Tunet took the hint and left.

29

It was early evening, six-thirty. In Dublin, Torrey, just off the bus, walked down busy Nassau Street and made a right into Dawson Street, and there was Waterstone's Bookshop. They were open until eight-thirty on Wednesdays, so she needn't hurry. And with five floors of books, they were bound to have what she was looking for.

Inside, she found the poetry section. Aisles of poetry, rows of slim books, fat books. Famous poets, infamous poets. She was at a section at the end of the alphabet. Yeats, Wilde, Williams, Tate, Wallace Stevens. She rounded a corner into another section . . . then another. Here, at last, were the *B*'s.

"Something I can help you with?"

Torrey smiled at the young woman clerk. "Do you have any poetry by Brannigan? Tom Brannigan. *Thomas* Brannigan?"

"Brannigan? Oh, *Bran*nigan! Absolutely! Right here. The book that just won the Halsey."

It was a handsome book with a blue cover, the title in gold letters.

"Only this one copy left," the clerk said, "you're in luck. We'll have to reorder. Anything else I can help you with?"

Torrey didn't answer. She held the volume of poetry in

both hands, looking down at it. She couldn't believe what she was seeing.

"Ma'am?"

Torrey, feeling in a trance, blinked, then looked up. "Oh! Oh, thanks. Sorry. No, thanks. This will do for now."

An hour later she got off the bus from Dublin on the access road, the bus driver obligingly having stopped at the break in the hedge. She stood a moment on the dark road. She somehow needed the stillness, the cold air. From above came the drone of a far-off plane. She looked up and saw the plane's light blinking. She moved her hand and felt the outline of the book in her shoulder bag. Then she blew out a breath that made a white fog in the air, and went through the break in the hedge.

There was a light on in the cottage. But Jasper was not there. Instead, she found a note on the kitchen table.

Off to Belfast. Damn the lot of them, both sides! This is the longest-running show extant. No other comment need apply. Ham in the oven, heart of my heart.

She hungrily ate the ham with bread and tea, then washed her hands thoroughly with soap so as not to get any grease spots on the book.

She read until ten o'clock at the kitchen table, turning the pages forward, then back, sometimes not actually reading but just looking up from the book and gazing off.

At eleven, she went to bed, first setting the clock for seven in the morning. The bus heading south on the access road would go past the break in the hedge about eight o'clock. She didn't want to miss it.

30

At Glasshill Hospital, Head Nurse Huddleson was barely starting her morning tea, and here was this young American woman, though visiting hours weren't until two o'clock. But since the young woman was so excited, having just read in a week-old copy of the *Irish Times* about the attack on the patient, Brannigan, and it seems he was a cousin of hers— Well, under the circumstances . . .

A nurse's aide in a blue uniform conducted the young woman to room 206. The patient was asleep. The young woman looked at the patient's bandaged head and bruised face. "How *dread*ful! Poor Tommy!" and to the nurse's aide, "I'll just sit here until he wakes up."

"Quite all right, I'm sure," the nurse's aide said sympathetically. "Nurse Huddleson will be in, in a bit."

"Thank you."

Torrey pulled the chair closer to the bed and sat down. She was taking the book from her shoulder bag when she knew suddenly that the man in the bed was watching at her.

"Poor Tommy," he mimicked her. His voice was husky; he cleared his throat. "Poor Tommy, indeed! A knight with a broken lance." A world of bitterness in his voice. It was a cul-

101

tured voice with a touch of brogue, just enough to bring it down to earth. His eyes were gray. He stared at her.

"Here in this cocoon, you wouldn't have heard," Torrey said. She hesitated, then plunged telling him who she was and pouring out the last ten days' events, beginning with the threatening phone call to Dakin at the groundsman's cottage and ending with the murder of Raphael Ricard at the cairn, with Natalie Cameron the suspect. Thomas Brannigan's eyes never left her face. His own face had begun to sweat.

"I'm here," Torrey finished, "because I don't believe Natalie Cameron killed that stranger from Canada. And I care about Dakin. And I think you can help. Because *you're* not a stranger, are you? Far from it, because—" She held up the book that had won the Halsey. Watching Tom Brannigan's face, she read the title aloud, " '*The Dakin Poems*.' "

Behind Torrey's chair, the door opened with a pneumatic hiss, a nurse's aide put her head in, said, "Oh, pardon!" and withdrew. Through the window from the other side of the hospital bed, came the sound of birds chirping. After a minute, Tom Brannigan at last said, "Well?"

"The poems," Torrey said, "reminded me of A. E Housman. *A Shropshire Lad*. Oh, not 'Terence, this is stupid stuff. You eat your victuals fast enough,' or 'About the woodlands I will go/To see the cherry hung with snow.' But lyrical, in that same way. Lyrical about a youth. But in *The Dakin Poems*, a boy is growing up. He's three years old. He's five. He's eight years old. And on." Torrey leaned forward. "All the stages of a lad's growing up, a loved child, in, say, a countryside like western Wicklow: the hills, the rushing streams, the mountainsides." Torrey paused, watching Tom Brannigan. "A boy who has a mother with hazel eyes and hair the color of honey."

A crash of dishes from the corridor. Someone swore, someone laughed. Torrey, holding the book, realized that her hands here clutching it as though she could wring something from it. In the hospital bed, Tom Brannigan slid his fingers along his brow, below the bandage that swathed his head. He closed his eyes.

Torrey said, "I see that each poem has the date when it was written, and where. Beginning fifteen years ago. All the poems were written in Montreal. Where you were living?"

A sigh. "Yes. This is the first—"

The pneumatic door hissed open. Nurse Huddleson, alert, face beaming, wiping the corners of her mouth for stray crumbs. "So! How does it feel, Mr. Brannigan? A visit from your cousin!" She looked more closely at the patient. "Perked you up, I can see that! A bit of color in your face! We'll call Inspector O'Hare in Ballynagh soon's Dr. Bascomb has a look at you." She turned to Torrey. "Your visit's done him a world of good, Ms . . . Ms . . . ?"

"Tunet." Torrey smiled back at Nurse Huddleson, who said, "Well, then!" The door hissed closed behind her.

Torrey said, "The date on that first poem. That would be when Dakin Cameron was only a year old."

Tom Brannigan lay back and gazed at the ceiling. He brought a hand to his bandaged head as though it head possibly contained too much to hold. Then, "My God!" followed by a strangled laugh. "Quite a journey you've made, Ms. Tunet! Delving, diving, discovering—hoping to save my Natalie! My Natalie, who is not mine! Can it be done? She had cause enough, God knows, for murder. But she never would have. Not Natalie! *Never*."

Torrey leaned forward. "Then help her! *Tell* me."

No sound, a stillness in the room, a hush that seemed to extend into the corridor outside the door; from the open window no twitter of a bird, no wind that fluttered a leaf. Then, from the bed, an enormous sigh.

"Back then," Tom Brannigan said, "I was twenty. Working on my father's farm in Drumcliff, County Sligo. The call came from my uncle Olin. Fill in, for a bit, chauffering at Sylvester Hall until he was up to it again, his kidneys all fixed. Better me, his nephew, than a stranger who might try to settle in for good, steal Olin's job. 'You'll go,' my father said. 'Save Olin's place for him. It'll expand your horizon, too, Tom. You'll have more to scribble about than farming in Drumcliff.' They laughed about my writing at night, but they were proud of it, especially my mother.

"So, Sylvester Hall. I arrived on a Friday noon. It was August. The housekeeper, Mrs. Dugan, had the second maid bring me out to the coach house, to where I'd stay, a room up above. On a hanger was my uncle Olin's summer uniform. Blue twill. It had been cleaned. I put it on. Too big in the waist, and I was taller, but it fitted well enough. Then I went down to look at the cars."

His voice stopped. After a moment, a sigh. "There were only two cars in the coach house. One I don't remember. Ordinary. The other was a silver Rolls. A Rolls! I'd seen only one Rolls in my life. It was in Galway, parked in front of the Great Southern, it had a diplomat's license. And now my second. Made me gasp.

"I got in the car. It felt strange. Here I was, the son of a farmer with a piece of land the size of my shoe, and I was sitting behind the wheel of a Rolls on a seat of the softest leather. The car's upholstery was green leather. The wood was polished walnut. The fittings gleamed. There were keys in a green marble ashtray on the dashboard. I poked about, looking for a manual, but I couldn't find one. I sat there trying to figure out what to push and pull. Then I heard a voice. Husky and laughing. 'There's a booklet in that little drawer, you press the button to make it open. Anyway, Mr. Chauffeur, I know how the bloody thing works.'

"It was Natalie. She got in the car beside me. Smelled like sweat, sweet sweat and horse sweat; she'd been riding. Hair in a tangle of curls, sunburn across her nose. Looked sixteen, which she wasn't, she was eighteen to my twenty. 'Shove over,' she told me, 'I'll show you.' Talked a blue streak, you'd have thought she'd taken a course in mechanics, what with all she knew. Slangy, too. Dirty mouth for a girl. I didn't know what to make of her. There was an open tin of tobacco in with the manual, my uncle Olin must've left it. Putting the manual back, I scratched my hand on it, the palm. 'Double shit!' she said, 'Poor lad!' and she ducked her head and licked it clean, her tongue on my palm. Then, like a joke, she pulled my hand up to her mouth and kissed the palm and laughed. 'Salty!' she said, 'Blood always is . . . red and salty.' At that I was—it was as though my head got turned around, I didn't know what. But something changed in me. I was never the same after that, right from the beginning. She was in my . . . my blood. And I in hers."

In the hospital room, Torrey looked at Thomas Brannigan's narrow, pale face. He had turned his head toward the window, but she had a sense that he was smiling. Gone was the cultured voice that over the years in Canada had become his. He had gone back, years back. The young chauffeur, telling his tale, spoke in the voice of the twenty-year-old from Drumcliff.

"All that August I'd drive her to Dublin in the Rolls to visit her great aunt in hospital. She wore a navy suit that was too small, she'd grown so. She had no dresses, only a white afternoon dress for proper social occasions and the suit 'for tea or the dentist in Dublin,' she told me, making a face, and a pair of jodhpurs for riding. The rest were school uniforms, but she'd graduated from her girls' school in June."

His voice drifted off, came back. "In Dublin, we'd eat sausages and mashed at a Bewley's. Then we'd wander around St. Stephen's Green or poke through bookshops. A bit of ice cream off a cart, sometimes. Then we'd drive back home to Ballynagh. But the fourth time we went to Dublin was different." Again he stopped, then went on:

"That fourth time, after Bewley's, Natalie wanted to go to shops, look in department stores, even buy something. But her allowance wasn't enough to buy more than a pencil case. I had my pay, but she wouldn't let me use it. She was in a daring mood, laughing and excited. We went to a shop where Natalie's great-aunt bought her school clothes, and Natalie bought a yellow party dress with flounces. Beautiful and expensive. She charged it to her great-aunt's account. She thought the manager would refuse or ask her questions. She almost didn't breathe, signing the charge. But they just thanked her and gave her the dress in a box, all in tissue paper. When we got outside with the box, she said, " 'I've been let out of school! In actu*ality*!' It was as though freedom from school and from her great-aunt in hospital had gone to her head, made her daring and wild. And she laughed so hard that people passing looked at her and couldn't help smiling.

"But in the Rolls driving back, she started to cry, so anguished I couldn't bear it. So I offered to let her drive, she'd never driven though she knew the manual by heart, she hadn't been allowed. The driving calmed her down. But that night she came to my room over the coach house."

Tom Brannigan rubbed a hand over his face and drew

an enormous breath. "She had on the yellow party dress. She'd put on lipstick. She stood looking at me. Then with the back of her hand she wiped off the lipstick and came to me."

31

At eleven o'clock Torrey got off the bus on the access road outside Ballynagh. The early morning sun had disappeared, the sky was overcast, a wind swirled the dry leaves about.

It would be at least a ten-minute walk to O'Sullivan's barn. But if she kept her hands in her windbreaker pockets they'd stay warm. And she had on her knitted cap, it covered her ears.

She tucked her chin deeper into her woolen turtle-necked sweater and started off. She didn't even see the woods around her, she didn't feel the cold, she was only hearing Tom Brannigan's voice, as he lay in the hospital bed.

"The old witch! I was chauffeur at Sylvester Hall for four months. Sybil Sylvester came home from hospital in September. I'd drive her to play bridge or to dine with her friends in surrounding great houses.

"Finally, Natalie and I knew we'd have to tell her we were going to get married. And that there'd be a baby. We were excited, happy. We had it planned. If it was a girl, we'd name her Millicent, for Natalie's mother. If it was a boy, we'd name him Dakin, after my father and grandfather.

"But then I had to go to Drumcliff for my older brother's wedding, I'd be gone two days. 'We'll tell her when you get back,' Natalie said. She was wild with joy.

"So I was gone two days. When I got back to Sylvester Hall, I threw my duffle into my room above the coach house and went to find her. But she wasn't anywhere about. No one, not the housekeeper, not the maids—*no* one knew were she was. I was bewildered. Then frightened. Natalie had known what time the bus was bringing me back to Ballynagh, she would have been waiting impatiently for me.

Finally, frantic, I burst in on Natalie's great-aunt Sybil in the drawing room. I'd never even been in that room before. Sybil Sylvester was playing solitaire at a gate-legged table near the fireplace.

" 'What's happened?' I said, 'Where's Natalie?'

"At that, Sybil Sylvester just looked at me as though I were too contemptible to be worth answering. Then she said, 'Natalie had a stomach upset. She confessed to me why. She wasn't even ashamed! What did she think? That I'd embrace the situation? Take you to my bosom? Pah! I explained to her that she'd been foolish, that you were only after the Sylvester holdings. That she must not see you again. That she must not have a child by you.'

"I was dazed. I must have gawked. And then she said, 'If you persist, if you think you can marry Natalie and live happily ever after—pah! I'll disinherit her. I'll leave her penniless. She'll get to hate you. Being a chauffeur's wife! A *Catholic* wife, besides, ending up with a gaggle of hungry brats! Living in some shabby public housing.' And she said, smirking, triumphant, 'I told her so. I painted a graphic picture for her.'

"I shrank from that. Sybil Sylvester sat watching me. She had blue eyes like agates, marble cold and shining, a doll's eyes. She was tapping the edge of a playing card on the table, her rings glittered.

"And she went on, watching me, 'Natalie didn't want to listen. But finally she knew I was right. You understand?

Natalie at last has understood. She has agreed not to see you again. She has already left Ireland. I have sent her abroad to some connections of mine. They will discreetly—they will take care of everything.' "

Torrey shivered, not only because of the wind that swept across the field as she approached the O'Sullivan's barn. She was seeing Tom Brannigan in the hospital bed. The edge of the bandage that swathed his head had darkened with sweat. "Gone. Natalie gone, leaving no word for me! But one thing that Sybil Sylvester had said rang in my head, the one thing I hated to think but it could happen: Natalie, penniless, trapped, could get to hate me, despise me. It was true she'd be better off without me. Comfortably off, rich, a secure life, marrying her own kind. And . . . maybe she'd gone because she wanted to keep on loving me! Loving me *forever and ever.* Was that a crazy way to think? Anyway, it's what I thought. *She loves me that much!*"

There in the hospital bed, Tom Brannigan turned his face fully to Torrey. "Sybil Sylvester was lying, of course, about what had happened to Natalie. But I didn't know it. Not then.

"And there in the drawing room, Sybil Sylvester's agate eyes watched me. And her voice was thin as vinegar.

" 'I have business connections in Canada. I can arrange a position for you. Clerking in a bank, in Montreal. At the Bank of Canada you will find five thousand pounds deposited to an account in your name.'

"When I left the drawing room, I could see Sybil Sylvester's reflection in the mirror over the mantle. She was laying down a new hand of solitaire.

"Upstairs in my room in the coach house I found a plane ticket lying on the table. A direct flight from Shannon to Montreal."

32

The BMW was parked in the rutted drive beside O'Sullivan's barn. Shivering in the cold, Torrey knocked hard on the barn door. "Kate!"

"Go away! I'm working!"

Oh, no! Let the world of art suffer. This was a matter of murder. Torrey pushed open the door and went in.

Kate Burnside was sitting on a swivel stool holding a mug. The easel before her was blank. What Kate Burnside had been working on was a glass of whiskey. The bottle was on the table beside her among a jumble of paint tubes. If Kate had been drinking hot rum, Torrey would have asked for the same. Her fingertips were ice cold. A cast-iron stove warmed the studio. Torrey blew on her cold hands and sat down on the arm of the leather sofa.

Kate Burnside, holding the glass, stared at her. "I said, *don't come in!*" Her voice was angry, a frown formed lines between her brows. She was wearing a heavy brocade kimono edged with what looked like sable. Her dark hair was in a single braid that was drawn forward over her shoulder and fell across her right breast. She looked romantic in a disheveled way.

Torrey said, "I'm sorry, but it's about Natalie Cameron. Because you were Natalie's friend. Her *best* friend. And—"

"Whoever told you that? Besides, it was a thousand years ago."

"All right. But while she's out on bail Inspector O'Hare is huffing and puffing, gathering evidence to get a conviction. I don't know what the penalty is in Ireland for murder, but it can't be pretty."

Kate Burnside swirled the drink in her glass and stared at her. "What's it *your* business? Just because Dakin got that phone call at your cottage. Yes, he told me about it. He tells me lots of things. Besides, Inspector O'Hare dislikes you. You *irritate* him."

Torrey said, "I've just come from Glasshill Hospital. I saw Tom Brannigan. He told me things."

No response. The only sound was the low roar of the stove. Then Kate said, "Went right to the fountainhead, did you?"

Torrey said, "You *were* best friends with Natalie, weren't you? Right up until you were seventeen or eighteen. Best friends. So you would've known about the chauffeur. Tom Brannigan. And that Natalie got pregnant with Dakin."

"That's none of your—"

"That's why Ricard was murdered, isn't it? *Because he knew.* And threatened to reveal it."

Kate Burnside said, "You *are* a tiger, aren't you?" She turned on the stool and uncapped the whiskey bottle on the table. "A libation?" Holding the bottle, she looked at Torrey.

"No, thanks. So. Blackmail. Of course!"

Kate filled her glass and recapped the bottle. Glass in hand, for a moment she sat looking back at Torrey and biting the inside of her cheek. Then she shrugged.

"Dakin came here that Thursday. He told me that Natalie had received two letters demanding money under threat of revealing something. But that Natalie had no idea *what.* Mystifying and frightening. Yet for some reason she was hesitating about going to the Gardai. That in itself alarmed Dakin even more. Poor lad! Struggling so with his bewilderment!"

"You were able to help him? You, his mother's old friend. Or not?"

"Not. It had become too complex. A Pandora's box. I didn't dare. Better to keep him in the dark, not knowing." She gave a sudden hoot of a laugh. "It was something that the blackmailer didn't know, either! It was something only *I* knew."

Torrey, on the arm of the leather couch, sat very still. "Knew?"

"Because I'd been there when it happened. Back then. I was seventeen. Natalie was eighteen. And in love with the chauffeur. Tom Brannigan."

"Knew what?" Torrey said.

"That second blackmail letter? Dakin told me that Natalie had refused to go to meet the blackmailer at the cairn."

"Yes?"

"So *I* went to meet him. I . . . well, not just because of what I knew that the blackmailer didn't know. But because I felt I owed Natalie something. In a way."

"Owed?" But then, when Kate only shrugged in response, Torrey remembered the mustard-colored jersey hanging in Kate's elegant bathroom.

Kate said, "So I went. That Saturday noon. I thought the blackmailer would be Tom Brannigan, come back from somewhere because he wanted money. I went to meet him at the cairn to tell him to let Natalie alone because she would never, ever, pay blackmail since she had no *idea* what he was talking about."

Torrey could only stare. She waited.

"But when I got to the cairn, it wasn't Tom Brannigan. It was this Rafe person." Kate put up a hand and touched the braid that fell across her breast. She pulled the brocade robe closer, the sable edging dark against her white throat. "Raphael Ricard, the papers say." She looked at Torrey. "I told him what I had come to tell Tom Brannigan."

"And what was that?"

"I told this Rafe person the truth. That Natalie had retrograde amnesia. She didn't remember that Tom Brannigan had ever existed. She actually thought Dakin was her son by Andrew Cameron."

33

It was a rainy evening," Kate Burnside said. "I had a party to go to in Dublin. My father was away, or he would have forbidden it. 'No daughter of mine'—and such-like drivel. 'You're only seventeen! Dublin is a sink of iniquity!' But my mother never could cope. I had a flame-colored dress and my parents had given me a little convertible when I'd graduated from Alcock's."

Telling it, Kate walked back and forth in the heavy, brocade kimono. She wore soft, thickly padded Oriental slippers that made no sound. She hardly glanced at Torrey, who had slid down from the arm of the sofa and sat among the cushions.

"Anyway, I kissed my mother and threw on a raincoat and went out. And there was Natalie just driving up in that big silver Rolls. "Get in!" she told me, her voice all queer. So I got in beside her. She sounded hysterical. She'd had a terrible quarrel with Sybil, her great-aunt. Sybil had found out about Tom Brannigan and that Natalie was pregnant. Sybil had been furious. 'Sleeping with the chauffeur! Like in some cheap sex film! Or like in that disgusting D. H. Lawrence's *Lady Chatterley's Lover*, sleeping with the gardener or whatever he was. And you're pregnant, besides. But you're *not* having this baby! We'll go abroad. I'll arrange everything.'

"In the Rolls, telling it, Natalie's face was white, she was wild with rage. 'How *dare* she! Tom and I—we love each other! We're going to get married!'

" 'Fine,' I told her. I looked out at the rain splashing down on the hood of the Rolls. 'Is there anything I can do? Just tell me. Anything. It's a shame! But I'm in a rush. I've a party to go to in Dublin.' And I said, 'D'you want to come?' "

" 'I'll drive you,' " she said, quick as a flash, 'It'll make Sybil wild to know I'm driving the Rolls. She's never allowed it. But I know how. Tom always lets me. And to Dublin! To a party! That's even worse.' And she laughed."

In the barn, Kate Burnside turned to Torrey and spread her hands helplessly. "I should have known better! And in that weather! But I was only a kid! And there was that party! By the time we got to Dublin, the wind was gusting, blowing the rain in sheets. We could barely see through the windshield, the streetlights were blurs. On Chancery Street we hit a curb and crashed into a streetlight.

"The accident was minor. Thank God for *that*, I remember thinking. Little did I know! Only a dented fender and a broken windshield and side window. But Natalie's arm was cut by broken glass. Luckily, the Gardai showed up right away, lights flashing.

"At the hospital, Natalie's damaged arm turned out to be a nasty business. Then it appeared that she also had a concussion. By that time, it was late, so staying overnight at the hospital was advisable for her.

"Aside from *that*, we had a problem with the Gardai: Natalie had no driver's license."

Kate, pacing, stopped in front of Torrey. "That cold-hearted Sybil Sylvester! The teachers at Alcock's Academy were angels compared to her. Well, anyway. I telephoned Sybil Sylvester from the hospital and told her about the accident. 'Indeed?' she said, her voice coming from somewhere north of Iceland. 'A fitting punishment! Running off in a temper! And driving the Rolls! Injured her arm? A deserved punishment! Don't expect me to rush off to Dublin and bring her home. She can take the bus. Feeling chastized if she has any sense. Not that she has shown much of *that*. As for the Rolls, I will see to the repairs. The cost will come out of Natalie's allowance.'

"I mentioned, then, feeling helpless and guilty, about Natalie driving without a license. To that, after a moment, she said, 'I am cognizant, Kate Burnside, of how to handle such affairs. It will be taken care of.' " Kate looked at Torrey. "She meant she knew people, she would pull strings. The license problem would quietly drop down a . . . an oubliette."

Pacing again, Kate began absentmindedly unplaiting her dark, luxuriant braid. "The accident was on Tuesday night. Natalie had mentioned that Tom Brannigan would be returning Wednesday morning from his brother's wedding in Drumcliff. 'We'll marry right away!' Natalie had told me, driving furiously through the rain toward Dublin, 'We'll be happy! I know it!'

"I'd taken the late bus back to Ballynagh on Tuesday night after the accident. So in the morning, Wednesday morning, I telephoned the hospital and learned that Natalie would be released in the late afternoon."

Kate Burnside took a deep breath and looked at Torrey. "It was my first encounter with evil. That is, if evil is *at all costs* to override everyone else's human feelings. Having her own way. I mean, of course, Sybil Sylvester.

"Anyway, Wednesday noontime I drove over to Sylvester Hall. I wanted to offer to drive Tom Brannigan to Dublin in the convertible to pick up Natalie at the hospital. But I couldn't find him. He wasn't upstairs in the coach house. The door to his room was partly open but he wasn't there. The room looked somehow so empty. Just nothing on the dresser, and no personal things about. There was only the chauffeur's uniform and cap on a hanger.

"At the hall, I found Mrs. Dugan, the housekeeper, in the kitchen and asked if she'd seen Tom Brannigan. She looked at me funny and said no. I had the feeling, though, that she was lying, that something was wrong and she didn't want to say.

"Anyway, at about three in the afternoon, not knowing where Tom Brannigan was, or what Sybil Sylvester had told him about the accident, if anything, I drove in to Dublin to pick up Natalie.

"It was a bright, beautiful, sunny day in early October, this time of year. At the hospital, Natalie was waiting in the reception room, her arm heavily bandaged. She was pale, but otherwise looked . . . she's really quite beautiful. And a nurse had brushed her butter-colored hair smooth, she couldn't have managed it with her one arm. 'I'm rather a mess, Kate,' she said. She looked down at her sweater, a coral sweater; it had a streak of grease on the shoulder. 'I'll never get that off!'

"I'd put the convertible top down, it was such a beautiful, breezy day, just warm enough. But the traffic was horrendous and noisy, and I had to pay attention to my driving, I'd had the convertible only two weeks. So it wasn't until we'd gotten onto Route N-eighty-one going south that we were able to talk. So I said—because I was a little puzzled, I couldn't think why Tom hadn't rushed to the hospital to see Natalie when he heard, unless—and it was a horrible thought—unless he didn't *know* about the accident! Maybe Sybil Sylvester hadn't told him! So I said to Natalie, there on the motorway, 'I went to the coach house this noon, looking for Tom. But I couldn't find him. I was a little worried.'

"At that, Natalie said, 'Tom?' And then again, sounding puzzled, 'Tom?' "

Kate stopped unbraiding her hair. She looked at Torrey. "I didn't understand. I said again to Natalie, *'Tom.'*

"She didn't answer. I risked a sideways look at her. There was a puzzled frown between her brows. Then she laughed. "Oh, the new hound! The pup! So they've named him? But what's wrong? He looked perfectly healthy yesterday. Or . . . was it yesterday? No, of course not! The day before?' She rubbed her forehead.

"At that, I was bewildered. There was no new pup. The last litter had been five months ago."

In the O'Sullivan's barn, Kate raised her shoulders, and hugged her arms, chilled. "You must understand, Ms. Tunet, I'd no idea. But I knew something was wrong. 'No,' I said to Natalie, 'Tom Brannigan.'

" 'Oh?' Natalie said, 'What have I missed? I've only been gone a couple of days! Or a day?' And she laughed and ran her hand along her bandaged arm. 'Who's this . . . Brannigan? You did say Brannigan.'

"It frightened me. I gripped the steering wheel hard, trying to hold on to reality: the car, the road, the traffic, the wind blowing our hair about. I didn't understand. I'd never heard of retrograde amnesia. Now I know it happens often with a concussion. A whole section of recent memory sheared off as though it were part of a cliff that falls into the sea. Something like that. Anyway . . . gone. But I was seventeen! I didn't know. I could hardly drive, I was so aghast. Tom Brannigan *no longer existed* in Natalie's mind.

"I left her at the steps of Sylvester Hall, I didn't want to go inside. I watched Natalie walk up the steps, that broad half-moon of granite steps. The door closed behind her. What had happened to Tom Brannigan? I didn't know."

34

Twenty minutes after leaving Kate Burnside, Torrey wheeled her bike down Butler Street. The village seemed unreal, made of pasteboard, an Irish picture postcard splashed with October colors. The reality was what she'd learned from Kate Burnside.

At Coyle's the Greengrocer's, she skirted the outdoor bins of squash and potatoes and inside she bought the asparagus Jasper had asked her to bring home; he was making asparagus on toast with a Mornay sauce of Gruyère cheese for their lunch. By now he'd have finished his "Jasper" column.

"Your change, Ms. Tunet."

"So," Torrey said to Jasper, who was sorting the stalks of asparagas at the sink, "at the cairn, Kate told Ricard that Natalie had retrograde amnesia and wouldn't remember that Tom Brannigan had ever existed. At that, Ricard laughed. He didn't believe her! 'What do you take me for?' he'd asked her, 'You're lying, you're just trying to protect your friend. That's it, isn't it?'

"And *then*, Jasper—here, use this towel. And *then* this Ricard character insisted to Kate that his extortion was more moral than Natalie's action in keeping Dakin's true patrimony a secret!"

Jasper, running cold water over the asparagus, gave a snort of laughter. "*Some*one was keeping Dakin's true patrimony a secret. Only it wasn't Natalie."

"What d'you mean?"

"After Natalie's accident with the Rolls, her great-aunt took her abroad on a trip to Italy, right? That's what you told me. Sybil Sylvester had plans. Quite frankly, an embryo had to be gotten rid of, an embryo of which its possessor, Natalie, was ignorant."

"Yes, that must've been what she—"

"But there was always the possibility that Natalie might get over her amnesia and remember Tom Brannigan. Then there'd be hell to pay."

"Ummm." Torrey nodded. "Sybil must've felt she was walking a high-wire. I can see that. Besides having to search out, and find, before too late—"

"Yes. But in Italy, she ran into a bit of luck. At their hotel in Florence they met Andrew Cameron. Good family, right religion, successful architect. And only thirty."

Torrey put an arm around Jasper's waist; he felt warm, solid, comforting. He was cutting up the Gruyère for the sauce. "Do go on."

"You'd have thought that the stiff-necked Sybil Sylvester would've disapproved of such a speedy romance. But she didn't. Not at all, my dear young friend. You can imagine why not."

"Without half trying."

"Indeed, Ms. Sybil couldn't have been happier. And she allowed Natalie to marry Andrew Cameron in a matter of weeks. Allowed? Likely she pushed it. Pushing Tom Brannigan out of the picture, for sure."

"Yes."

"From what I've picked up in the village, Andrew Cameron

was a handsome, strong-hearted, loving gem from Scotland. So Natalie was lucky, there."

Torrey was silent, watching the steam begin to rise from the skillet. She was thinking how at Sylvester Hall there'd been a dictatorial progenitor who looked like a porcelain doll with a rosebud mouth, and who dined out and played bridge and guarded a secret. She said, "Jasper, Kate Burnside mentioned that Sybil Sylvester died when Dakin was about eight years old. What's that saying in the Bible about 'Bread eaten in secret is pleasant'? So for more than eight years Sybil Sylvester had her pleasant-tasting bread."

At three-thirty, Jasper left for Dublin, where he had an editorial meeting. Leaving, he turned in the doorway. "Did Kate Burnside say how that blackmailing bastard knew that Tom Brannigan was Dakin's father?"

Torrey shook her head. "Kate said she'd asked him and he'd only said, 'When hard-pressed, you can always find a golden egg.'"

"Or a slashed throat," Jasper said. The door closed behind him.

Alone, after some minutes, Torrey got up and took the jump rope from the hook beside the door. She pushed the kitchen chair out of the way and began skipping rope. It would steady her.

But almost at once the phone rang. Myra Schwartz calling from Interpreters International, the Boston office. "Torrey? Don't you ever check your E-mail? Did you get my message?"

"Oh, no. Actually, I've been—" She stopped. *Been getting myself entangled in a murder case.* "Sorry, Myra. What's up?"

"Money, honey." Myra never wasted words in the one language she spoke, which was pure American. "A back-to-back assignment: Russia, directly after Budapest. October twenty-eighth. Five days, same Eastern European payment. Ginny will arrange the flights. What *about* that?"

"Yes. Terrific." She dropped the jump rope, picked up a pen from her desk, and scrawled notes about the Department of Commerce, Rossya Hotel, Moscow.

When she hung up, she looked at the calendar on her desk. Budapest was six days from now. As for Moscow, luckily her Russian was fluent, she wouldn't have to buckle down for that, just a bit of vocabulary concerning commerce. And a smidgen of Georges Simenon. Even so, time was short.

Dakin.

Was it because of Dakin that, against all odds, and making no sense, she stubbornly wanted to believe that Natalie Cameron was not the killer of her blackmailer?

"Well, yes," Torrey said aloud. "Now that you ask." From the top kitchen drawer she took out a chocolate bar with almonds. Tearing off the silver paper, she sat down at the kitchen table to think.

35

In the upstairs west hallway at Sylvester Hall, Jessie said, "Dakin? I seem to have found this key. Can't think what it belongs to. So old and all! It was just lying there beside the grandfather clock."

Dakin stopped; he'd been on his way downstairs. He took the key from Jessie. Antique sort of thing, thin, lacy looking. Could be the key to the escritoire opposite the grandfather clock, that seventeen-century escritoire with the inlaid kidskin top. "Let's see." He fitted the key into the lock and turned it. At once, a click. "That's it, Jessie. Thanks. I'll give the key to my mother."

Jessie gone, he stood holding the key. He wasn't going to look for his mother. He knew where she would be: in that dim corner in the old coach with its four-sided, beveled-glass lamps. She had, lately, a dreaming face; an *elsewhere* face, as he thought of it. Always before, she'd been *there*, attuned to him. Now she seemed to hesitate over even calling him by name. It bewildered him. He remembered that once, in his happy childhood days, when he'd been eight or nine, he'd asked her, "Why am I named Dakin? Is it from Daddy's family? Or from your side?"

"Neither," she'd told him, smiling. "I don't know why. It

124

just sprang to my mind when you were born. When they put you in my arms, I said, 'Here's Dakin! Here he is!' "

He looked down at the key in his hand. He felt as unsteady as though the earth had shuddered under his feet. Next month his mother would have been marrying Marshall West, whom she loved. But instead she'd be indicted for the murder of the blackmailer. Motive unknown.

Dakin sat down on the top step of the great staircase and put his head in his hands.

36

"Nurse Huddleson? Inspector O'Hare here. How's our patient? Brannigan. Tom Brannigan. Conscious and lucid enough for me to—*What?* A relapse? His cousin? This morning?"

Two minutes later, Inspector O'Hare slammed down the receiver. "God∂amn it!"

Sergeant Jimmy Bryson looked up. He was sitting on the bench beside the door, blacking his shoes. Nelson was snoozing at his feet. It was five o'clock Thursday afternoon.

Inspector O'Hare said, "A young woman claiming to be Tom Brannigan's cousin showed up at Glasshill Hospital ten o'clock this morning. Blather, blather, blather, the two of them, Exhausted him, he's out of it again. A young woman, *claiming*—"

"Her," Jimmy Bryson said. "Torrey Tunet."

"Of course. Slim, with a pixie face, big gray eyes, all excited about—god∂amn it!"

"Obstructing justice," Sergeant Bryson said. He carefully ran the blacking sponge around the edge of the sole. It made all the difference in the look.

"We've no grounds for arresting her." O'Hare said. "We never have."

"Always mixing in," Sergeant Bryson said. He blacked the

heel. "That old chest in my uncle Frank's storeroom? Ms. Plant says I should take a picture of it and send it to Sotheby's. Could be worth something, she thinks. Sometimes they'll put a photograph in their brochure for an auction, she says. She says they take about a third, their share. Christie's, too. Same thing."

Ms. Plant! Ms. Plant! O'Hare was sick of hearing what Ms. Plant said, believed, and knew. She was supposed to leave today for the antiques show in Cork, and he'd thought, Godspeed! Or the devil speed her. Whomever. But unfortunately, Monday evening, after dinner at Finney's with Sergeant Bryson, she'd turned her ankle on the cobbled street. A bad sprain, it turned out, lots of swelling. She couldn't drive, not for several days. Her rented Saab was parked out back of Nolan's. Sergeant Bryson was sympathetic, and in O'Hare's view, too damned attentive. Twice his age. Almost. As O'Hare had said to Noreen last night, "I thought that was more in France, a young man and an older woman. "*Chéri,*" Noreen had answered, "Colette. It was a book. And what about Helen Lavery's sister, Maeve, forty, and married to the younger Forrest boy, twenty-six? So there you are."

The phone rang. In his stocking feet, Bryson went to his desk, answered, and turned to Inspector O'Hare. "Gilbert Sanders, forensics at Dublin Castle."

Inspector O'Hare pressed the button and picked up his phone. "Gilly?" He listened. "Yes . . . yes. Thanks, Gilly." He put down the phone, shook his head, and blew out an exasperated breath. First, Ms. Tunet at Glasshill Hospital, and now this! Newsmongers like the *Daily Mirror* and the *Irish Sun* would delight in blowing it up big. His phone would be ringing every two minutes. Bad enough that photographers and journalists were already showing up in Ballynagh. "Damn them all! I've a job to do!" But at least it would soon be over: within the month, Natalie Cameron would be indicted for murder.

"Something up, Inspector?" Bryson was giving him his alert, intelligent look, that birddog look.

"Nothing that'll send the apples spilling out of the cart, Jimmy. Dublin Castle has the report on the murder weapon. The penknife. Natalie Cameron's fingerprints on it, of course. And Ricard's. But at some time two other people handled that penknife. Unidentified fingerprints. We'll check out Dakin Cameron."

37

Nurse Huddleson? This is Ms. Tunet, Tom Brannigan's cousin. I hope he's better since yesterday, I'm planning to visit him again as soon as—Oh, Inspector O'Hare? Did he? Well, actually, cousins by *marr*iage, his sister married my—A relapse? I'm so sorry! No visitors, under the circum—? I'll call again in a day or so to see when I can—Oh, I see. Inspector O'Hare. Well, thank you anyway, Nurse Huddleson."

Torrey hung up the phone with such an angry jerk that the phone cord knocked over her teacup. Tea spilled across the kitchen table and down onto her jeans. Damn it, altogether!

But mopping the tea from the table, she couldn't help suddenly grinning. O'Hare's face would have gotten red with anger when he'd learned of her visit to Glasshill Hospital, his gray-white eyebrows would have bristled, he'd have used that darling Sergeant Bryson as a sounding board to his rage. "That meddler!" he'd have grated out to Jimmy Bryson. And he'd have added a few other choice and unrepeatable words regarding that snoop, Ms. Torrey Tunet.

"Well, too *bad*, Inspector," Torrey said aloud. But minutes later, in the bedroom, changing into her only other pair of jeans, she'd thought, with chagrin, *So close. So close!* In the hospital, voices outside in the corridor when before leaving, she'd asked Tom Brannigan, "Who struck you down? Who could have done it?"

On the coverlet, Tom Brannigan's hands had clenched. His voice was bitter. "A man I hate! He must've seen my name on the register at Nolan's. So he'd've known I had come. And why. The *bas*tard! Ricard's his name."

He'd have known I had come. And why. At that, Torrey had leaned toward the hospital bed. She only half heard the crack of approaching footsteps in the corridor. "Why *did* you come back?" she asked, but the door was opening, Nurse Huddleson and the harrassed-looking young doctor came in. Nurse Huddleson looked discomfited, the doctor's face looked grim. "*No* exceptions! *No* determinations made by staff members!" he was saying over his shoulder to Nurse Huddleson, "Visitors' hours only! *As stated*. A hell of a way to run a. . . ." and so on.

Two minutes later, Torrey, chagrined, was standing at the bus stop outside the Glasshill Hospital, thinking, *Why?* Why *had* Tom Brannigan come back? Never mind! Tomorrow she'd return here for the answer.

So she had thought! But now! *Now* Inspector O'Hare had talked to Grasshill Hospital and destroyed her chance of learning anything more from Tom Brannigan. She'd be barred from visiting him. Still —

A man I hate. He must have seen my name on the register, so he'd have known I'd come.

The register. Nolan's Bed and Breakfast.

38

Panting a little from the stairs, Sara Hobbs, owner and manager of Nolan's Bed and Breakfast, came into the small parlor that served as the reception room. Ms. Brenda Plant was sitting in one of the rattan basket chairs that was, to Sara's mind, exactly right against the rose-patterned wallpaper that Sara loved. She'd chosen the wallpaper herself, and Brian, her husband, had put it up.

"Ms. Plant? Here's the magazine, October issue. Hern's Newspaper Shop had it. So *lucky*! It was the last copy!" Sara handed the magazine *Body Beautiful* to Ms. Plant. On the way back from Hern's, she'd read the titles of the stories: *Keep-Your-Curves Workout. You Can Be Svelte and Strong. Hoop Exercises to Music. Eat Meat or Not?*

"Thank you, Mrs. Hobbs." Ms. Plant wore a cowl-necked cashmere sweater, almost the shade of her heavily mascaraed blue eyes. Her beige pants hid the bandage on her ankle from Monday night's sprain.

Sara looked admiringly at Ms. Plant. She was really a handsome woman, with that full figure, and the red hair, dyed likely, but she had the right, hadn't she? Fine posture, too. Kept her shoulders back. Unconsciously, Sara straightened. Brian nagged her a bit about her posture. She was forty-five, about Ms. Plant's age.

The wall clock behind the desk chimed the noon hour. "So *late!*" Sara clicked her tongue. "And I haven't half done the rooms! I expect Sergeant Bryson will be along for you any minute."

Ms. Plant gave the tiniest sigh. "I expect so."

Sara Hobbs gone, Brenda Plant riffled the pages of the magazine. Hardly a minute alone since that accident at the gates of Sylvester Hall! Sara Hobbs acting like a guardian angel. And Sergeant Jimmy Bryson, always at her heels, protective as a rottweiler guard dog.

It had been like living in a glass bubble. She itched to leave Ballynagh. And now the bad luck of turning her ankle. Her ankles were her one vulnerable spot. She wouldn't budge from Ballynagh until it was fully healed.

As for Sergeant Bryson's attentions, obviously there wasn't enough crime in Ballynagh to keep Sergeant Bryson busy. And now he'd become infatuated with antiques. And with her! He was even upset that she'd miss the antiques show in Cork because of her ankle. He'd hinted that he'd been planning to ask Inspector O'Hare for a day off to accompany her to Cork. Really, now!

Still, the infatuation of a man of twenty-four was pleasurable. A dozen years ago, men of Sergeant Bryson's age were falling all over her. And she was even now in fine physical shape. She ate wisely and did her exercises every day, no slackening. Probably she was in better shape than Sergeant Jimmy Bryson himself, or than that Ms. Tunet, always on her bicycle. Or the deep-breathing Winifred Moore who'd go striding through the woods as though on an elephant hunt.

Brenda Plant pulled in her stomach. She opened her magazine.

In five minutes, she was so deeply intent that she didn't hear the quick, light footsteps of someone on the stairs.

Coming into the little parlor, Torrey stopped short, annoyed at seeing Brenda Plant sitting there over a magazine. She'd somehow expected to find the room empty. She slanted a glance toward the flat-topped table where the guest register lay. Relax. Just *relax*. She forced a smile. "Hello, Ms. Plant."

Ms. Plant gave a startled jerk and looked up. "Oh! I didn't hear you!" A pencil she was holding over the open magazine slipped from between her fingers and fell to the carpet.

"Sorry." Torrey picked up the pencil and handed it to Ms. Plant.

"That's all right."

Torrey said, lying, "I was looking for Sara Hobbs, is she about? I wanted—"

But someone was whistling, coming up the stairs. An instant later Sergeant Jimmy Bryson appeared, uniform immaculate, buttons gleaming, shoes mirror bright. Probably, Torrey thought, he'd even polished the face of his wristwatch.

"Well, now! Ms. Tunet!" Sergeant Bryson's eyebrows went up in surprise, but he gave her only a glance before turning to Brenda Plant. "Ready, Ms. Plant? I've brought the cane. And you can just lean on me." He glanced back at Torrey. "The antiques auction in Dunlavin. There's an Irish credenza, circa 1850. I'm going to bid on it if Ms. Plant thinks it's worth it. I can't go too high, though."

"Good luck," Torrey said. She suppressed a smile. Jimmy Bryson passionate over antiques. And apparently over Brenda Plant. She watched them leave, Ms. Plant leaning heavily on Sergeant Bryson to favor her good ankle, Sergeant Bryson looking like he'd found the Holy Grail.

A pity, Torrey thought. Minutes ago on Butler Street, she'd seen eighteen-year-old Hannah, Jimmy Bryson's girl-friend, going into Miss Amelia's Tea Shoppe. Hannah had looked pale and unhappy.

Alone, Torrey went immediately to the guest register. She leafed quickly back through the pages. Brannigan . . . Brannigan. Ah, here! Tom Brannigan, middle of the page. Arrived Saturday, a week ago, around noontime, no earlier, no later. Sara Hobbs always noted, in parentheses, time of arrival. So . . . within two hours of his arrival, Brannigan had been struck down at the gates of Sylvester Hall. *By a man I hate. A Canadian. Ricard's his name.*

Torrey leafed farther back, day by day: Saturday, Friday, Thursday Wednesday, Tuesday, Monday—ah! Monday. Raphael Ricard. So Ricard had arrived in Ballynagh six days earlier than Tom Brannigan. Six days during which this Raphael Ricard had been attempting to blackmail Natalie Cameron. Blackmailing her until he got his throat slashed.

Torrey crossed to the rattan chair and sank down. She rubbed her forehead. Natalie Cameron, since being out on bail, had not set foot outside of Sylvester Hall. Too many photographers from gossip magazines lurked about the gates to the hall and sat in cars along Butler Street, eating sandwiches from Finney's. So Jessie did the shopping, with a list from Breda, the cook. Dakin was currently working on the Piersons' roof. Luce after school made a beeline for Dakin, wherever he was working.

"Why, Ms. Tunet!" Sara Hobbs, pulling off an apron, bustled into the parlor. "So nice to see you!" Her eyebrows went high, questioning. Torrey said, easily, "I just stopped in to see—I'm wondering, Ms. Hobbs—When you're cleaning up, ashtrays, for instance, in any of the guest rooms—have you noticed any cigarette butts that're a Sinbad brand?"

"Cigarette butts? *Ash*trays? Mother of God, no! No smoking at Nolan's. A notice is posted in every bedroom. Brian has to smoke out in the garden. *Sinbad?* Never heard of that one. Why?"

"Oh . . . I just wanted to know where they're available. An American friend of mine likes them and doesn't know where to get them in Ireland. I thought maybe one of your guests could tell me."

Sara Hobbs, taking off her apron, said, "Good to see you anyway, Ms. Tunet. Since you're here, can you stay a minute? So's I can just run down and get the post?"

"Of course," Torrey said. Sara Hobbs was one of her favorite people in all of Ballynagh, never mind that Sara's idea of afternoon tea was two glasses of sherry and interminable reminiscences of her childhood and the Mediterranean ship's cruise she and Brian Hobbs had taken on their honeymoon twenty-two years ago.

Waiting, Torrey picked up *Body Beautiful,* an American magazine, which lay on the end table beside the chair. It was what Ms. Plant had been reading. She'd turned down the corner of a page. Torrey opened to the page. It had an article on the benefits of exercise for women. At the bottom of the page was an ad: *"The Roslina Exercise Method. Three Videotapes: Raise your Breasts; Narrow Your Waist; The Perfect Stance."* Ms. Plant had made a penciled checkmark beside the ad and had doodled on the ad itself.

"There!" Panting from the stairs, Sara Hobbs laid the bundle of mail on the desk. "Thank you *so* much, Ms. Tunet."

"Not at all." Torrey put the magazine back on the end table.

39

It had rained since early morning. At Grasshill Hospital, by the two o'clock visiting hour, it was pouring hard, there were flashes of lightning and the rumble of thunder.

The visitor splashed his way in from the parking lot. Once inside, he shrugged out of his raincoat and walked down the corridor to Nurse Huddleson's desk.

"Nurse Huddleson?"

She looked up. The visitor handed her his card. Reading it, Nurse Huddleson's eyes widened. Jasper Shaw. Jasper *Shaw!* The investigative reporter for the *Irish Independent.* The Omaga massacre. The Veronica Guerin murder. The Cavan drug exposure. The Ulrich shipping revelations.

"Visiting Tom Brannigan." Mr. Shaw had a deep baritone. He could be a romantic-lead movie star if he lost a dozen pounds and had a full head of that dark, curly hair that rimmed the back of his head. Nurse Huddleson patted her own blond chignon.

"Tom Brannigan," Mr. Shaw said again. Nurse Huddleson felt a thrill of excitement. Was there an important story in Mr. Brannigan? Surely Jasper Shaw wouldn't be here otherwise!

But . . . Inspector O'Hare? If it came to *that!* Surely, though, Inspector O'Hare had meant only that the young woman, Ms. Tunet wasn't to be allowed to visit Mr. Brannigan. Surely that's what Inspector O'Hare had meant. Only Ms. Tunet. Surely. And it was visiting hours, two-fifteen right now.

Nurse Huddleson conducted Jasper Shaw down the corridor to room 312.

A half hour later, while Nurse Huddleson was going over charts on her desk, Jasper Shaw's baritone voice above her, said, "Thank you, Nurse Huddleson."

She looked up only in time to catch a flash of his dark blue eyes, then the raincoat swirled around his shoulders and he was gone.

It was four o'clock. In Ballynach the rain had stopped. At the groundsman's cottage, rain dripped from the eaves. Inside the door, Jasper hung his raincoat on the hook.

"Did you get it?" Torrey asked. She surreptitiously slid the burned scones into the garbage under the sink. She'd made them as a teatime surprise. But instead, they'd have the brown soda bread Jasper had baked yesterday. She'd toast it, and there were sardines and butter and jam.

"Yup." Jasper said. "Brannigan shuffled around a bit, then broke." He took the tape from his raincoat pocket and slid it into the cassette player on Torrey's desk. "What's that burnt smell?" He was grinning. "I've a taste for my twenty-minute drop biscuits." He was already at the flour bin, whistling under his breath.

Torrey sank down at her desk and turned on the tape. A whirring sound. Then Tom Brannigan's voice, already stronger than yesterday.

"Ricard. I didn't trust him or distrust him. At first, he was only someone who'd drop in and browse among the books in The Citadel. That's a bookshop I owned. To understand what happened, the ugliness of it, I have to go back to when I first came to Canada. So you'll understand. Because I followed Ricard to Ireland to kill him."

Listening, Torrey could see the twenty-year-old Tom Brannigan living in a third-floor walk-up in Montreal. She saw him at work in a teller's cage at the Bank of Canada wearing a white shirt and gray dust jacket. Evenings, heartsick, he sat at a table in the little flat writing long letters to Natalie, then tearing them up.

"All I had of Natalie was the one keepsake she'd given me: her father's ivory penknife. Nothing else except a little charm bracelet with three dangling unicorns I'd bought her. She loved it, but she'd broken the clasp. She'd given it to me to fix."

Miserable, aching for Natalie, he'd begun attending one of the evening writing classes offered at McGill. "Since I was a kid, I'd been scribbling poems. So I thought, why not? It was something to escape to." Meanwhile, he didn't touch the five thousand pounds that Sybil Sylvester had banked in his name. "The thought of using it disgusted me."

He ate indifferent meals in coffee shops. Daily he bought the *Irish Times* and the *Independent*, never missing an issue. "I inched over the pages, always hoping to see something about Natalie. I was starved for word of her.

"Word of Natalie! A bitter news item, when it came! The announcement of her marriage to Andrew Cameron within a month after I'd left for Canada! It near destroyed me."

No sound now on the tape. Torrey leaned forward and saw that the tape was still turning. She waited. Then, at last, again Brannigan's voice.

"But what happened next was much worse. Or as I came to think of it later, when my brain could finally handle it, a world lost. A whole world lost!"

In the *Irish Times*, within a year of his arrival in Montreal, he saw in the list of birth announcements, "Born, to Natalie Sylvester Cameron and Andrew Cameron, a son, christened Dakin."

"That's when I knew. I walked around my room like a crazy man, laughing and crying. Sybil Sylvester had lied to me! The baby was mine! Natalie had named the baby Dakin, just as we'd planned! Dakin was our name for the baby if it was a boy. Dakin was my father's and grandfather's name. *Dakin!*

"So Natalie was married to Andrew Cameron but they had *my* baby."

The cassette stopped. Torrey, stunned at what she was hearing, popped out the tape and turned it over. Brannigan's voice yearned back toward that lost world.

"What had Natalie's great-aunt told her? Likely that I'd abandoned her. That given the choice of money, or of a struggling life of poverty with her, I'd chosen the money."

On the tape, startlingly, a woman's cheerful voice: "Ten minutes more, Mr. Shaw. Visits are limited to a half hour." Then Jasper's voice, "Right you are, Nurse," and the pneumatic closing of a door followed by a momentary silence. Then Tom Brannigan.

"That's when I started writing the Dakin poems. Several appeared in little magazines. Gradually, over the years, they accumulated."

So uneven, Tom Brannigan's voice, unfolding his tale. Now, besides reading the Dublin papers, he got subscriptions to newspapers in Wicklow. Over the years he read that Andrew Cameron and his six-year-old son, Dakin, won a trout-fishing contest; that Dakin Cameron, aged ten, was playing doubles in a junior championship tennis match in Bray; that thirteen-year-old Dakin Cameron had come in third in a county school spelling contest.

"I read that another child was born to Natalie and Andrew Cameron. A girl, they'd named her Lucinda." He clipped the items from the papers.

Meanwhile, he opened The Citadel Bookshop. The bookshop was a success. It gained a reputation for an eclectic selection of literature. Tom Brannigan moved into an expensive flat on Wheelock Street. The Citadel took up all his time, he had acquaintances rather than friends. His solace was in books. "I preferred it that way. To read. To write. To dream."

But then—

"Two years ago, at breakfast I opened the *Irish Times* and read that Andrew Cameron had been killed in a drug-related cross fire in Dublin."

At once, he'd fantasized going back to Ballynagh. He would go to Sylvester Hall, he would go up the avenue to the hall—"No, I'd go to the coach house. Natalie would be there. We would look at each other. Natalie would say . . . But then I thought, 'Too late, too late!' "

A silence. Then the clink of a glass, and Jasper's voice. "Take a sip. It's still cold. You'll be all right."

A pause. Then—"Thanks. I thought, finally, 'Give up. It's done. It's over.' But then! *Then,* a month ago *The Dakin Poems* won the Halsey Prize. I could hardly take it in. The Halsey! And I suddenly became encouraged again.

"I *would* go back! At once! I remember laughing out loud. I was reaching for the phone when I happened to look down at the *Irish Times* and saw, among the social announcements, the engagement of Natalie Sylvester Cameron to the architect Marshall West."

Behind Torrey, Jasper said, "Turn it off. Better have your tea before you hear the rest of it. Or you might lose your appetite."

"Why? Is it bloody?" She turned off the cassette.

"Worse. It's Raphael Ricard."

40

W inifred," Sheila said, "I'm having nightmares. That man is the first dead person I've ever seen. He looked *horr*ible! We're actually involved in a *mur*der! I can't get it through my head. We're *wit*nesses. All because of mushrooms! Not that we ever found even one single mushroom. I've always admired Natalie Cameron. I'll hate having to testify that Natalie killed—"

"Sheila, please! We didn't actually *see* Natalie Cameron kill that man. And there's no explanation as to why she would've done it. It's only circumstantial."

They were in the sitting room at Castle Moore, close to the fire after a high tea, the kind Winifred loved, "hearty meat stuff," Winifred called it.

Sheila, crouched on the hassock, was nervously unraveling the fringe, as usual. Winifred had almost given up trying to stop her. The hassock had taken on a moth-eaten quality. Two more visits of Sheila from London, and it would be bare of fringe.

"Ma'am?" It was Hannah, tray in hand, come to clear the table. "There's a call from Inspector O'Hare."

Winifred glanced at the red light blinking on the phone next to her elbow. Then she looked keenly at Hannah. The girl's face was pale, as pale as her silky long fair hair. It was her night off, so why wasn't she getting dressed up to go to the movie in Dunlavin with Sergeant Jimmy Bryson? Winifred frowned and picked up the phone.

"Inspector?" She was gazing after Hannah, who was clearing away the tea things on the table in the window embrasure. "Good afternoon, Inspector. Yes? Yes. Our statements? Of course. We'll be in tomorrow morning."

"What?" Sheila asked, when Winifred put down the phone.

"Inspector O'Hare would like us to come in and sign the statements we gave him on tape. What we saw, the blood and guts. He's got to extract the juice from the bones of this killing at the cairn."

Sheila made a face. "What an unappetizing way to put it, Winifred!" Sheila shuddered and pulled at the fringe on the hassock.

Winifred said, "O'Hare wants a total package to deliver to Dublin Castle. And to RTE, the *Dublin Times*, the *Independent*, the *Daily Mirror*, the *Irish Sun*. And maybe even the *Sporting News* under—"

"Winifred, *how* can you be so ma*cabre*?"

"A family trait. It came with the castle. For God's sake, Sheila, leave that fringe alone!"

41

Dusk showed purple through the cottage windows. Jasper, poking up the fire, said, "I'll clear the table, you go ahead. It's on the same tape." Passing behind Torrey, who was taking a last sip of tea at the kitchen table, he leaned down and kissed the top of her head. "You'll find more than one surprise."

Torrey got up, stretched widely, and went to her desk in the corner. She sat down and clicked on the tape. She folded her arms, leaned back, and listened again to Tom Brannigan's voice.

"Rafe Ricard. A financial advisor. Obviously rich and successful, from the clothes he wore: British-made suits, the Patek watch, Italian leather shoes. He'd drop in often at The Citadel. He'd talk a lot about the importance of making knowledgeable investments.

"The success of *Citadel* had been written up in *Business News*, so I wondered if he was angling to get me as a customer. Several times he invited me out for a drink. I never went, I'm allergic to alcohol and I'd rather handle my own investments. Besides, there was something about this Raphael Ricard . . . something I didn't quite trust."

Then one evening, Tom Brannigan's doorbell had rung. "It was that terrible evening. I had just read the announcement of Natalie's engagement to Marshall West."

Numb, wretched, he'd gotten out his scrapbook of Dakin's growing up, his school sports prizes, his trips with his father. "His *supposed* father." Beside it lay a copy of *The Dakin Poems*. He was crouched over the coffee table, heartsick, turning over the pages of the scrapbook.

"It was then that the doorbell rang. I answered the door, I thought it was the superintendent come about the chimney down draft.

"It was Rafe Ricard. He came in, laughing, hearty, in a sheepskin coat, carrying a gift-wrapped bottle of cognac. He said he was celebrating, that he'd just made a fortune in international investments. 'We're having a drink, then I'm taking you to dinner,' he said, as though we were intimate friends.

"Can you guess? I thirsted for that drink! I poured it myself, filling the glass. Rafe Ricard looked surprised. But I could tell that it pleased him to see me drink. He walked about, talking investments, saying that I was wasting my money by not getting professional financial advice. Then, crushing out a cigarette, he noticed the scrapbook on the coffee table. 'Who's the kid? Your son?' He was half joking. But I couldn't help it. 'Yes! My son!' And I poured another drink. I was shaking."

The voice on the tape stopped. Torrey leaned forward, but the tape was still turning. Then, a cough. A sigh. Brannigan's voice came again, thin and bleak.

"When I awoke, it was morning. I was sprawled in a chair next to the coffee table. Within minutes I was violently sick. Did I tell you I was allergic to alcohol? I managed to shower and dress, I would have to get to the hospital. But on the way out, passing the coffee table, I saw that my scrapbook of Dakin was gone.

"Then I realized that the copy of *The Dakin Poems* was also missing. So was the *Irish Independent*, which I'd folded back to the engagements announcements.

"Slowly I turned to the mantel where I kept the penknife and the little unicorn bracelet. They were gone as well.

"I began to recall going to pieces and drunkenly sobbing and babbling out to Rafe Ricard the miserable tale and my mistake in leaving Ireland. I heard myself saying, 'The old woman lied to me! I knew that, when I learned that Natalie had named her baby Dakin.'

"Sick as I was, and knowing the alcohol would soon make me deathly ill, I found Ricard's number in the phone book and called him. I was out of my head. A recording machine answered, saying he was out of town, please leave a message. The message I left was that I was going to kill him. I rushed out and took a cab to his apartment, I was too sick to drive.

"His apartment was on Redfirm Avenue, very elegant. When I asked for Mr. Ricard, the doorman told me that Mr. Ricard was out of town.

" 'He can't be!' I shouted at the doorman. 'I was with Mr. Ricard last night! Call him!'

" 'I'm sorry, sir,' the doorman told me. 'Calm yourself. Mr. Ricard took a cab to the airport an hour ago. I called the cab for him myself. I heard him tell the driver, "Aer Lingus." ' "

Torrey clicked off the tape. "The bastard! The absolutely living-end *bas*tard!" She looked across to Jasper, who was sitting at the kitchen table, tapping on his laptop, writing his culinary column.

He looked up. "We could use a bit of jolly Irish conviviality to rinse out the taste of Raphael Ricard. Best accomplished at O'Malley's over a pint. Then we'll be dining right here at eight. Candlelight, wine, and a mystery dish. You're my guinea pig. Finish with that cassette—if you can stomach it—and we'll be off." He rubbed his hands and went back to the laptop.

Torrey clicked on the tape. "The allergy put me in the hospital. I was there for five days. My assistant took over at The Citadel. When I got home from the hospital, I packed a bag. My plan was simple, Mr. — Mr. — ?"

"Shaw. Jasper Shaw."

"Mr. Shaw. You already know what I came to Ireland to do."

42

At seven o'clock, when Torrey and Jasper left the cottage, it was cold and clear. A silver dime of a moon shone down. They skirted the little pond, went through the break in the hedge, and onto the access road. It was only a fifteen-minute walk to the village, but the cold went clear to the bone. Torrey had pulled on her knitted navy cap, it covered her ears. She wore jeans and a heavy jacket over her flannel shirt. Jasper, in pants and his oatmeal sweater, was bare-headed on the theory that the cold weather would help him shiver off some of his fat.

Butler Street was empty, their footsteps sounded loud on the pavement. Beyond Nolan's Bed and Breakfast were the lighted windows of O'Malley's Pub.

"Jasper?" Torrey slowed and put a hand on Jasper's arm. "I didn't ask you, but how did Tom Brannigan know it was Ricard who struck him down?"

"I asked Brannigan that. It's not on the cassette because the tape ran out. Poor planning for a hot-shot investigative reporter, right? Chagrin. I hadn't expected Brannigan to break and tell me so much."

"Well, how'd he know that it was Ricard?"

"There's only one bed and breakfast in Ballynagh. Nolan's. Tom Brannigan guessed that the gabby Sara Hobbs naturally

148

would've mentioned to Ricard that another guest from Montreal had arrived. So Ricard would've checked the register and—"

"And he would've seen Tom Brannigan's name."

"Right. So then Ricard knew it was a no-choice-but-murder game."

In O'Malley's, there was firelight and loud Irish traditional music from a group of three boys led by Fred, Sean O'Malley's second son. At the crowded bar, Jasper wedged himself far enough in to order the beers. Torrey unzipped her jacket and breathed in the smell of beer, old wood, and cigarette smoke. Someone jostled her, but she managed not to spill even a drop from the foam-topped glass that Jasper handed back to her over somebody's head. It was all a kind of conviviality that soothed her. It tamped her down. She felt she needed the relief of it after hearing Tom Brannigan's unnerving revelations. She was glad to be here.

Glass in hand, she wandered to stand beside the fire; the tables were all filled, some with diners, most with folks chatting or drowsing over drinks. The television was on above the bar, but hardly heard except by those clustered there to hear it. A soccer game was in progress, bare-kneed lads in striped shirts running here and there, bruising each other inadvertently or otherwise. An occasional cheer went up from the bar.

In a few minutes Jasper joined her, pint in hand, a third of the glass already gone. He said, voice low, "Much after the fact, but thought I'd check. Sean O'Malley likely thinks I'm onto illegal shipments of cigarettes. He says he never heard of Sinbad cigarettes or even saw such a cigarette butt. He gave me a funny look."

"Yes?" Torrey hardly heard. She was gazing in bemusement at the soccer game, one of the bare-kneed boys had

149

made a goal. A cheer went up, and someone at the bar raised a glass high and waved it wildly about. Someone she knew.

Twenty minutes later, on their way out past the bar, Torrey paused to greet him. "Mr. O'Boyle! Hello! I saw the shrubs from McGarrey's all set in at Sylvester Hall along the road. Wonderful! Just what was needed, I thought. But a few, each side of the gates, are taller. Why's that?"

"For the look," Sean O'Boyle said. "That's for the look, for when I cut it. A kind of swoop up, it'll be like a curve." He blushed, the color coming up from his throat. He was unshaven and the neck of his sweater was greasy.

Outside of O'Malley's, Torrey drew deep breaths of the cold, clear air. "I'm an air junkie, hooked on the ozone of Ballynagh."

"Move over, there's a car coming," Jasper said.

An old silver Rolls drew up beside them and slowed. "Ms. Tunet? Hello!" Natalie Cameron was at the wheel. Lights from O'Malley's windows shone onto the street, and onto Natalie Cameron's sweatered arm that rested on the car door. "Do you want a lift? I'm going past the cottage."

"Thanks, but no," Torrey said. "You're talking to a pair of exercise addicts."

"Well, then . . ." Natalie Cameron raised her arm and flicked her fingers good-bye. In the yellow light from O'Malley's, something glittered on her wrist, something dangled.

They walked on. Torrey, stunned, said, "Did you see it?" She could hardly take it in. There had been no sound, but what she saw was a thunderclap.

"The bracelet? Yes. I saw. Unicorns."

"But I don't—Where could she have gotten it from?"

"I can guess," Jasper said. He was taking such long strides, it was hard to keep up. "That blackmailing bastard, Ricard, must have sent it to her. He stole it from Tom Brannigan's apartment, didn't he? So sending it to Natalie along with her father's penknife would be his way of telling her that he knew about Tom Brannigan. So hand over the money."

Torrey said, "But if Natalie's now wearing that bracelet, that means *she must have finally remembered.*"

Jasper said, "I'd say so."

Walking, they had reached the access road. It was only a few minutes now to the cottage. The night was clear and it was no colder than when they'd left O'Malley's. Yet Torrey felt that even her bones had turned to ice. She said, "The vital—the important thing is, Jasper, exactly *when* did Natalie Cameron remember about Tom Brannigan? And that Dakin was his child."

"Ah," Jasper said, approvingly. "I see what you mean." He put an arm around Torrey's shoulders. "Maybe Natalie remembered soon enough for her to go to meet Ricard at the cairn, bringing not the blackmail money but a rage to kill him and keep her secret."

Torrey felt a tremor, the dark woods along the road tipped and righted. She wouldn't give up. *Connaître le dessous des cartes.* She'd discover the undersides of the cards. She'd push on. But in what direction? Think. *Think!*

151

43

At 2:45, the school bus from Marlow's Girls School stopped at the corner above Coyle's vegetable market across from Nolan's Bed and Breakfast. Three of the teenaged girls who got off started up Butler Street together, chatting and laughing, hunching their shoulders against a brisk wind.

"Marcy? Marcy McGann?" Torrey, waiting in the lane beside Corey's, stepped out into their path. Marcy was easy to recognize, her bushy red hair was almost orange and it came down to the shoulders of her navy parka, the same parka she'd been wearing when she and Willie Hern had been near-witnesses to the clubbing of Tom Brannigan. She had a broad, pretty, freckled face. She said, uncertainly, "Ms. Tunet?"

"Yes. I was waiting. Can we talk for a minute? Is that all right?"

In Miss Amelia's Tea Shoppe, Marcy McGann put her books on the floor, shrugged out of the parka, sat down, and in the next half hour consumed three cups of tea, one scone, one cherry muffin, and two medium-sized cinnamon-topped buns, talking all the while. It had been scary, what with the woman in the green coat screaming, and then running, and the man's bloody head. She and Willie talked a lot about it. Willie said it was gypsies, they'd wanted to rob the Canadian, but the woman's screaming had frightened them away. "Of course it doesn't half compare to that murder at the cairn. Still . . ."

"But Marcy, you didn't *see* any gypsies?" and when Marcy shook her head, "What exactly *did* you see?"

"Well, I saw *you*, Ms. Tunet. I saw you coming on your bike. And I saw Ms. Plant, like I said. She was across the road from the Sylvesters' gate, so of course she could see what was happening at the gate. Enough to make *any*one scream! Willie said she sounded like a fire engine. Inspector O'Hare has it all down on paper. Just the way Willie and I told him." Marcy licked a finger and pushed it around on the plate among the crumbs and cinnamon and sugar, then sucked her finger. She gave Torrey a sidelong look, and giggled. "Except for the bird. Inspector O'Hare would've thought I was a rattle brain."

"The bird?"

"A blue jay, I'd thought at first. Flying low. Disoriented, maybe. Anyway, likely must've bashed itself on a tree or something. Like they sometimes do, I guess. Its body is probably lying there decayed already. Willie agreed that that wasn't what Inspector O'Hare was after hearing, anyway."

Torrey sat gazing at Marcy. "So that was all? You could see the road and the iron gate, of course, and—"

"Oh, no," Marcy said. "We couldn't see the gate or anything the other side of it, if that's what you mean. The roadside trees were in the way. So that was all." She poked at a crumb on her plate. "It was exciting, though. Like being in a film."

Torrey sat gazing at Marcy. Then she smiled at her. "Another muffin?"

For some minutes after Marcy McGann had picked up her schoolbooks and left Miss Amelia's, Torrey sat. She was, for one thing, actually wishing that Myra Schwartz at Interpreters International would call her to say that the Hungarian assignment had been rescheduled for a later date. But why? The fragments of information from Marcy McGann by themselves meant little, had given her nothing to pursue. True, one of them had, for a moment, stopped her. It was related to something Torrey had seen or heard. When? Where? She knew it was recently. Yesterday? Today? Tantalizing not to recall. But if she inched her way back, event by event, she'd find it. It was the same as when, having misplaced her keys, she'd—

Ah! Ah, yes! Yes! "*That* was it!" she said aloud. She'd been curious, had meant to follow up. But things had intervened—Jasper with Tom Brannigan's tale. Then something nagging at her about Sean O'Boyle.

But Marcy's mention of the blue jay reminded her that when she'd gone to search around the Sylvester gates, she'd been interrupted by Sean O'Boyle and never had poked about. She looked at her watch. Just four o'clock. Why not now?

"Ma'am? Another pot? That one's gone cold."

"No, thanks, you can give me the bill."

44

It was dim in the coach house, the afternoon was cloudy and light shone weakly through the high, dusty windows. There was a smell of mold near the grindstone.

Sean, holding the blade of the shears against the whirring stone, realized that the smell came from a drip in the roof that had rotted one of the old bits of harness that hung on the wall.

That harness! He laughed suddenly, remembering his first years here. Once, Natalie, nine years old, had stood on a box and taken down that same harness. She'd ineptly harnessed Ms. Sybil's skittish mare to it and gone careening over the south meadow until she'd ended afoul a rock and knocked out a tooth. It had torn her school uniform, too. Ms. Sybil had had Natalie pay for a new uniform out of her weekly allowance until it was all paid up. It made Sean hate Ms. Sybil. No. Despise her. Sean had then secretly hired Natalie to help him plant seedlings in the greenhouse. He'd paid her out of his earnings to make up for her lost allowance. Natalie had loved their secret. They still had a special smile between them, though he was sure she must have long ago forgotten why.

Sean left the coach house and brought the sharpened shears around to the greenhouse against next week's pruning. Then he started down the avenue to have a look at the new shrubs along the gates. Partway there, he took out his pocket comb and combed his hair, sleeking it up the sides with his palm. It was for himself, not for anybody else. How he looked to himself. It was why he always walked so straight. As though he were seeing himself, his reflection. As in a mirror. Or a pool.

He was more than halfway to the gates when he glimpsed something moving along the road down past the shrubs. Not a rabbit or a dog, a somebody.

Weeks ago, he would have just kept on. But now there was violence and death. There'd already been too much that threatened those at Sylvester Hall.

So he stepped from the crunchy gravel to the grass and approached the road more quietly. Now, partly screened by the new shrubbery and the iron gates, he could see.

It was someone, their back to him, bent over, and picking up something from among the brambles. Someone in old jeans and a tan parka. She was whistling under her breath, "The Lion Sleeps Tonight." Ms. Torrey Tunet.

Just then, Ms. Tunet suddenly broke off her whistling. "Well, now! Do tell!" She was holding something, but because she was half turned away, he couldn't see what. She pulled a man-sized handkerchief from the pocket of her parka, said, "Sorry, Jasper," and wrapped whatever it was in the handkerchief and dropped it into the pocket of her parka.

Sean watched as she got on her bicycle. She was whistling again as she bicycled back along the road to Ballynagh.

45

Tuesday morning, Torrey's alarm clock went off at six o'clock. It was a brisk, sunny, blue-sky day. Torrey turned off the alarm and immediately got up.

For the next three hours, dressed in jeans and a flannel shirt, she did various things: She rearranged all of Jasper's herbs on the kitchen shelf. She jumped rope for half an hour. She read the second Simenon book in Hungarian, not taking in who had shot the lawyer's wife or why the wife had had an affair with the druggist in the first place. She swallowed a cup of coffee and a heavily buttered piece of brown soda bread. She glanced at the clock on the dresser at least twenty times.

At nine o'clock she pulled her heavy V-necked raspberry sweater on over her shirt. Outside, she got on the Peugeot.

At Nolan's Bed and Breakfast, by nine-thirty, breakfast was over. The tourists in rooms 3 and 4 had already departed with their luggage. So only three rooms were now occupied; their occupants had gone off fishing, antiquing, driving about, or browsing the one souvenir shop in the village.

Brian Hobbs, Sara's husband, was making up the rooms. Norah, the help, was down with a cold, and Sara was off at O'Curry's Meats for the sale on pork shoulders. Brian had the vacuum out and the room doors open, he had just finished room 5 when he saw Ms. Tunet coming down the hall. Behind the scenes, so to speak. Ms. Tunet had a bit of dash to her, the way she held her head; and those gray eyes, this morning, had a touch of violet beneath them, as though she hadn't slept well.

Clearly Ms. Tunet was wanting to speak to him. Noisy vacuum. He switched it off so they could talk. Turned out she'd come to ask him about some kind of cigarettes she wanted to buy. Sinbads. She knew he smoked, she wondered if he knew where she could get some Sinbads.

"Sinbads?" He shook his head. "Never heard of them."

Miss Tunet said, "Well, thanks, anyway." She looked curiously about. "That Canadian who was murdered. Was that his room?" She was looking toward room 5. Brian shook his head. "No, the Canadian fellow was in room Two. We had to keep it locked for a week—tourists curious, and all."

"And Ms. Plant's? Curious about hers too? Room three, isn't it?"

Brian shook his head. "No, she's room five."

"Well . . . I guess no luck about the Sinbads," Ms. Tunet said. "Ah, well." She wiggled her fingers at him and he turned on the vacuum again and went into room 2. He thought she'd left, so it startled him when ten minutes later he came out of room 2 and there she was, just outside in the hall. It made him jump. She smiled at him and said something about having lost a button off her flannel shirt and thought maybe in the hall. But the way her gaze slid away, he remembered suddenly what the village had found out last year about Ms. Torrey Tunet having been a thief. But of course she'd been a kid, in her teens. He'd done a few things himself he didn't like to remember and which would've shocked Sara if she'd known. The past was past. Anyway, about doing the cleaning, he ought to lock each door after he finished the room, not just go from room to room to save time to have a cigarette out in the garden. Sinbad cigarettes? He shook his head.

It was ten o'clock. Lucinda knocked on the cottage door. No answer. Sun filtered through the trees and shone down. Birds chirped in the hedge. Otherwise, silence. Lucinda hesitated, then knocked again. Still nothing, nobody. What to do? Maybe Ms. Tunet would come back soon. She'd wait. She *needed* to see Ms. Tunet. She sighed and resettled her brimmed cap.

Waiting, she squatted beside the rather mucky pond. She was poking at a little frog in the sun on a flat rock at the edge of the pond when minutes later she heard someone whistling, and Ms. Tunet came through the hedge, pushing her bicycle. Ms. Tunet looked . . . *brilliant*, somehow. Tired, but *brilliant*, her cheeks stained with extra color, her gray eyes like they'd just seen a bunch of fireworks explode right in front of her face. She blinked when she saw Lucinda. "Lucinda! Hello! I've been wanting visitors. Come in."

Lucinda hesitated. For a moment she felt uncertain, maybe it was a mistake to come, maybe she'd make some excuse, back away, and leave. But then, of course, she couldn't. Because she had to try. She pulled at the bill of her cap and waited while Ms. Tunet unlocked the door.

Inside, there was barely a gleam from a peat fire in the kitchen fireplace, but it was warm enough. Ms. Tunet said, "Take off your things, Lucinda. My heavens! It's so cold outside, I got chilled. I could use a cup of hot cocoa. How about you?" She yawned but she still had that brilliant look.

"I suppose," Lucinda said. "Thank you." She unzipped her parka and edged onto one of the kitchen chairs. One thing, she wasn't going to cry.

Making the cocoa, Ms. Tunet kept looking at the directions on the can and spilling things, and talking at her over her shoulder. Lucinda could tell that Ms. Tunet was trying to chat about subjects interesting to children: the new litter of kittens at Castle Moore, this Saturday's jumble sale at Dunfy's farm with toys advertised; *Little Women* coming up again on Sunday on television. Lucinda took a deep, quivering breath, she didn't care about any of that right now, not even Jo in *Little Women*. She sat pushing the salt and pepper shakers back and forth.

Ms. Tunet poured the cocoa into the mugs, set the mugs on the table, and said with relief, "There!" as though she'd just climbed a mountain. She sat down and looked across the table at Lucinda. Her voice was gentle. "What, Lucinda? What is it?"

"I'm so *worr*ied, Ms. Tunet."

"Worried, Lucinda?" Ms. Tunet stirred her cocoa.

"About my mother." Lucinda forced herself not to cry. "I'm not *against* anybody, and I don't want to just be spreading ugly stuff. You know?"

"Well, actually, I'm not sure what you mean, Lucinda." Ms. Tunet blew on her cocoa. "Ugly stuff?"

Lucinda put her hands around her mug to warm them. "You were so brave when you grabbed that telephone from Dakin! So I thought maybe you'd know what I should do. That's what I came for. Though the cocoa is *very* good."

"Thank you, Lucinda."

"So maybe if I told *you*, it would be different. Because *official* people think children make up things to be important, and it gets innocent people into trouble. I mean official people like Inspector O'Hare might think so, if I told him. Though of course it's sometimes the case. The actual case."

"Ummmm. I guess that's so, Lucinda."

"Inspector O'Hare is a very nice man, actually. But you know how the Gardai are. Sometimes. In their zeal. I'm *for* the Gardai, naturally. Where would a civilized society *be* without the Gardai. But I'm worried sick. And telling *you* about . . . about *it* is different from spreading it."

"Spreading what, Lucinda?" Ms. Tunet said. "What you're here about?"

"Well . . ." Lucinda took a deep, quavering breath.

Five minutes later, her tale ended, Lucinda sat with her hands clasped to her chest. "Will it help my mother?"

Ms. Tunet was staring at her. "It might. It just might." Her voice was a little breathless. "I'm glad you came to me. And for now, best not to go to Inspector O'Hare."

"All right."

Lucinda drew an enormous breath of relief. She had a feeling she could trust Ms. Tunet to do *some*thing. What, she didn't know. She got up and put on her parka and gave her billed cap a yank. Ms. Tunet accompanied her outside. But before they went out, Ms. Tunet took a Polaroid camera from the dresser drawer, saying she wanted to take some outdoor pictures of the cottage. She was just in time, too, because when they came out the sky was already getting cloudy. Dark clouds were massing over the mountains west of Ballynagh; the sun still shone but it was going to storm, one of those rainstorms that turned the village streets into rivers.

Lucinda skirted the little pond and went through the break in the hedge.

46

It was a deluge. Black clouds, then the downpour, the wind slicing through it, all so sudden that the lunchtime crowd at Finney's was pretty well trapped inside.

Winifred Moore, sitting across from Sheila at a window-side table, pulled the ecru curtain aside, looked out, and at once ordered a second dessert. The ice cream with banana and nuts. "No sense in going out in *that*," she said to Sheila.

It was, peculiarly, as though a kind of homey, family peace descended on the restaurant. Terence, who worked at Lowry's Hardware and was always in a hurry, sat back and relaxed. One of the O'Dowd brothers told about a cow who walked backward when it stormed. He swore it was true. The butcher, Dennis O'Curry, told his favorite old chestnut. It was how, twenty years ago, he'd triumphed over the late Sybil Sylvester. It was about the time she'd paid his bill for six lamb chops and included a nasty note: "Mr. O'Curry! I can get lamb chops in Doyle's for a pound less. I only ordered them from you this past Thursday because Doyle's is closed on Thursdays." Dennis, after mulling this over, meanwhile downing two whiskeys at O'Malley's, had sent the bill back to Sybil Sylvester, having scrawled on it, "When I'm closed I charge a pound less than Doyle's." Everybody laughed at that one.

Winifred, starting on her second dessert, noticed that Sergeant Jimmy Bryson, at the next table with Ms. Plant, wasn't having his usual favorite: corned beef with mustard and pickles. Instead, he was eating Finney's all-vegetable jumble, as was Ms. Plant. He was messing it around a lot; but Ms. Plant seemed to be enjoying hers. Winifred leaned over to Sheila. "Who's running *whose* young life?"

Sheila followed her glance; then gave her a reproving look. "Is it any of *your* business who eats what?" Sheila was still smarting over *l'affaire champignon*, as Winifred called it. Sheila now even refused to eat mushroom anything, even mushroom soup that came in a can.

A blast of wind shook the plate glass window and the slanting rain struck it with a sound like peas rattling into a pan. At that instant the door opened and Torrey Tunet came in. Old leather air pilot's hat tight to her head, her face wet. She wore a red slicker buckled high around her neck. And as Winifred said later to Sheila, "Up to something, as usual!" "Of course!" Sheila had answered, "But *then*, who would've guessed?" and she gave a little shudder.

"Torrey!" Winifred waved her dessert spoon at Torrey. "Over here! Join us."

Torrey gave a nod and flicked her fingers in response. She unbuckled the red slicker, and hung it on one of the row of hooks that was already overloaded. She came over, smiling, pulling off the pilot's cap. "Hello! The whole village must be here." She nodded to Ms. Plant and Sergeant Bryson at the next table. Bryson was fiddling with a green bean, turning it this way and that on his fork.

Torrey pulled back one of the two empty chairs at Winifred's and Sheila's table and sat down. "I saw you through the window, I only came in to say hello and to show you something. Look at these!" She pulled an envelope from her shoulder bag and fanned out a half dozen photographs.

"Shots of the groundsman's cottage. I took them early this morning. Sunny and springlike, can you believe it? My instant camera. I'm not an expert photographer like you are. But I think they're pretty good for an amateur. What do you think?"

Winifred looked down at the photograph Torrey handed her. Awful. Worse than amateurish. Couldn't Torrey see that? She looked at Torrey. What could she say? *Very nice?* Or something more honest, like, *Throw away the camera?*

But Torrey was leaning over to Jimmy Bryson at the next table. "You've always liked the cottage, Sergeant Bryson. Have a look," and she dropped a couple of photos on the table and smiled at Brenda Plant. "You, too, Ms. Plant. You like old things, antiques and such. The cottage is certainly that. Look at this one, it's my best," and she handed Ms. Plant a photograph.

Winifred spooning up the last bit of banana, glanced at Torrey. Something. A tenseness. Torrey's gray eyes, were a fraction wider than usual; a pulse was beating on the side of her neck just above her cowl-necked sweater. Something up. All was not as it seemed. Puzzling. Well, never mind. "The rain's stopped," she said to Sheila. "Let's go." And to Torrey, "I've got the Jeep. Can we give you a lift anywhere?"

"Perfect," Torrey said. "You can drop me at the turnoff to O'Sullivan's barn. It's on your way." She gathered up the photographs that Sergeant Bryson and Ms. Plant had laid on the table after murmuring polite comments. She slid them into the envelope and got up.

It was a mist rather than a drizzle by the time the Jeep reached the turnoff to O'Sullivan's barn. Standing in the dirt road, Torrey watched the Jeep disappear, mud splashing up around the wheels. Then she turned and walked up toward the barn.

The blue BMW was parked in its usual place. It was only two o'clock, but the day was dark. Lights shone from the high windows.

Torrey went to the BMW and opened the car door. Smell of perfume, tobacco, stale whiskey. In a holder attached to the dashboard was an empty glass. Baccarat. Wouldn't you know! She had to smile. Carefully, between two fingers, Torrey lifted out the glass. "Once a thief, always a thief," she whispered aloud, and made a face. She took a paper bag from the pocket of her raincoat and put the glass in the bag.

47

Oh, no! No! Inspector O'Hare stared at Ms. Torrey Tunet standing in front of his desk and taking an object from her shoulder bag and placing it on his desk . . . then reaching into the bag again and taking out another object, which she placed beside it. Then a third object. *Oh, no!* Yet here she was. Had he committed some sin in an earlier life to deserve her meddling *again*?

Ms. Tunet was in a red slicker and a close-fitting World War I leather pilot's cap she must have found at a yard sale. It was three o'clock and the sudden noontime deluge had dwindled to a drizzle. She smiled at him. "Inspector."

The fourth thing she took from her shoulder bag was a chocolate bar. She made an inquiring gesture as though to break it in half, and when O'Hare shook his head in refusal, she peeled back the silver paper and bit into the chocolate. She unbuckled the red raincoat and sat down in the chair beside his desk.

Inspector O'Hare set his jaw in his *no* mode. He folded his arms and swore to himself that this time, *this* time, whatever theory Ms. Torrey Tunet came up with, *this* time it would slide off him slick as oil. She'd get nowhere.

Nowhere. Because this time was different. He knew what he knew: Natalie Cameron had killed Raphael Ricard. He had two eyes. He didn't need a third one in the middle of his forehead to confirm that fact.

Ms. Tunet said, "Inspector," and she reached across and picked up one of the objects she'd laid on his desk and began to talk.

Twenty minutes later, Sergeant Bryson returned from the Harrington's farm, having settled a fistfight between the seventy-eight-year-old Harrington twin brothers over which puppies in their bitch's new litter would belong to which brother. He found Inspector O'Hare alone sitting at his desk, biting the inside of his cheek, and gazing at some things that lay on his desk.

Bryson said, "All settled, Inspector." He felt good, pleased with himself. "After Henry got a black eye and Stevie lost a tooth. There were five pups, so who was to get the odd one? I felt like King Solomon."

"Hmmm? King Solomon?" Inspector O'Hare gave a sudden bark of a laugh. "Which one did get it, Jimmy?"

"I did, sir. Cost me thirty pounds. When it's weaned, I'll pick it up. My mother'll like it, she's been wanting company." Bryson took off his cap and rubbed his forehead and looked over at a packaged doughnut he'd left on his desk. "Wouldn't mind a bit of tea, though a mite early."

"Sergeant Bryson."

Bryson felt suddenly alert. Something in the Inspector's voice. "Sir?"

Inspector O'Hare said, "Never mind tea. I want you to take these things"—he gestured at the objects on his desk— "right now to Dublin Castle, forensics. I've already rung up Sanders. Depending on what he finds, I may be calling an informal meeting. If so, Friday morning at ten o'clock."

48

I swear," Jessie said to Sean O'Boyle, "today's a false spring. That balmy!" Jessie was wearing only a light jumper over her white-aproned blue uniform. She was standing on the gravel on the curved drive in front of Sylvester Hall watching Sean O'Boyle trim the masses of rhododendrons beneath the long windows. She'd come out to gather up some of the cuttings of the shiny leaves. They'd look a treat in the brass pots in the kitchen.

It was Thursday morning, eleven o'clock. Sean, only half aware of Jessie, had already finished trimming the rhododendrons on the left side beneath the drawing room and breakfast room windows. Minutes ago, he'd begin to trim those on the left, beneath the library windows, which were open, and from which he could hear the murmur of voices. Ms. Tunet's bicycle was on its stand on the gravel drive. It had been there at least twenty minutes.

"Jessie?" Ms. Cameron had come out and was standing at the top of the steps. "Jessie, will you please get Dakin for me. He's in the coach house washing the Rover. Tell him I'm in the library and I'd like to see him."

"Yes, Ma'am." Jessie went off toward the coach house, the gravel crunching under her feet.

Sean paused in his clipping and looked up to where

168

Natalie still stood at the top of the steps. She had on a long velvety-looking brown skirt and a brown pullover and her face looked pale, so different from its usual warmth. At that moment, she put her fingertips to her temples, closed her eyes, and shook her head slowly from side to side. Then she opened her eyes, blew out a breath, and turned and went inside.

Sean just stood for a moment, shears in hand. It was terrible, Natalie's face so thin these last days. In the greenhouse, even while he showed her what cuttings he was taking, and while she replanted one thing or another, or looked at him when he was explaining something about mixtures of soil, her hazel eyes had a transfixed look as though her gaze was frozen on something.

Meantime, those gossip reporters were prowling around the Sylvester Hall gates and in Ballynagh having a pint in O'Malley's and chatting up young Sean O'Malley as though he were privy to secret goings-on at Sylvester Hall. As for Dakin, he'd given up doing jobs around Ballynagh, what with people plaguing him with questions about his mother. Natalie's attorney, Mr. Morton, had come from Dublin three times and had left frowning, his jaw set. The inquiry would be next week, in Dublin.

A smell of coffee wafted from the library window, and again the murmur of voices.

Ms. Tunet had arrived almost a half hour ago. "She called around ten o'clock," Jessie had told Sean while he was doing the rhododendrons that had begun to tower over the sills of the breakfast room windows. It was something to do with a meeting tomorrow morning at the Garda station. "Ring! Ring! That telephone!" Jessie had said. Earlier, it had been Sergeant Jimmy Bryson calling. "Yes, Sergeant Bryson, Ten o'clock, Friday morning?" Natalie had said. Nothing got past Jessie.

"Hey, Sean." From behind him, Dakin's voice. " 'What bodes the day?' Did Shakespeare say that or did I make it up?"

Sean turned, smiling. Dakin wasn't even wearing a jacket. Just jeans, and a jersey with the sleeves rolled up for washing the jeep. It was one of his batch of mustard-colored jerseys that he'd bought from a catalogue. This one had a raccoon on it.

"I think you made it up," Sean said. Not that he had any idea.

When Dakin went inside, Sean didn't start clipping again. Holding a rhododendron leaf and rubbing its shiny, dark green surface, he just stood there beneath the open library window, head cocked, listening to the voices.

49

At eight o'clock Friday morning, Jasper picked up the phone in his bedroom suite at the Actons Hotel in Kinsale and dialed Torrey's number in Ballynagh.

He was sitting on the edge of the bed, already dressed. Crew-necked black sweater, white pants, and sneakers. In the tipped bureau mirror on the left side the room, he could see the reflection of the harbor; the sea glittered in the morning sunlight; yachts and sailboats and other small craft seemed barely to move. On the bedside table beside him lay the program for the ten-day International Gourmet Festival at Kinsale, the gourmet capital of Ireland. He'd arrived last night from Dublin, driving south on the N9 in the Jaguar. He'd dined at Kieran's on the celebrated roast wild boar, but his taste buds had betrayed him. He could have been eating Styrofoam.

"Torrey?" But it was her machine that answered, her familiar "Torrey here. You're calling the right number . . . at the wrong time —" only then to be picked up. "Hello?"

"Torrey?" He grinned. She would be in that long striped flannel shirt she wore as a nightgown. Yawning, half-awake despite the cold water dashed on her face, she'd be in the kitchen taking his shaped biscuits from the refrigerator and baking them, maybe even remembering to let the butter get —

"Jasper? Jasper! Hel*lo*." Suprise and pleasure in her voice.

He said, "You're sabotaging my taste buds. I keep seeing you sleuthing away. My investigative nature—"

"Jasper, listen." Torrey's voice was sober. "Since you left, I've been tracking through a labyrinth that the Minotaur himself could get lost in. Then, by a sheer fluke . . ."

While she told him, he gazed out at the sunlit harbor. The yachts and small craft seemed to take on an innocence that had not been there before.

"So," Torrey was saying now, "when I started to tell Inspector O'Hare, he got that exasperated, stay-off-my-turf look. Then gradually as I talked, I could tell he thought I was simply crackers. *Fin*ally, he began to take it in, thank God. So then he started wiggling that tough jaw of his around that way—you know how he does—then I guess he figured he couldn't risk ignoring it. So, 'Better run it past Dublin Castle.' Right?"

Jasper, bemused, said, "Right."

"Just in case I wasn't a total idiot. So then, when yesterday he got the report back from forensics at Dublin Castle, he called for an informal meeting at the Garda station."

"When?"

"This morning, ten o'clock. I've still got to dress and have breakfast. I keep wishing you were here. Jasper?"

"Yes?"

Torrey's voice was serious, sad. "If I'm right about what happened—You know that expression, 'unalloyed joy'? Is it ever possible? In real life, no matter how delicious the apple, there's always a worm. Twice in the past, I've uncovered the truth behind a murder. And each time it has exposed . . . each time there's been a cruel price that somebody, innocent but entangled, had to pay. In this case, it'll be Natalie Cameron.

The exposure. A pity. But there's no other way. And then, of course . . . Dakin."

Jasper, gazing out at the sunlit harbor, said, "Yes, that. The son." He was thinking hard.

"Jasper?"

"I'm still here." He paused, then: "All of a sudden I find myself wearing my Jasper Shaw investigative reporter hat. Tell me again. What was it that Kate Burnside told you about that Rolls Royce trip to Dublin, the two girls, Kate Burnside and Natalie Cameron?"

She told him. Then, "Why? What're you thinking?"

"I don't know yet." And he didn't; it was too elusive. But out there somewhere. He said, "And what about Tom Brannigan? What's going on with him?"

"I don't know. Because up to now Grasshill wouldn't tell me anything about his condition. They had orders from Inspector O'Hare to treat me like yellow fever."

After they hung up, Jasper sat for some minutes, thinking. Then abruptly he reached out to the bedside table, picked up the program of the International Gourmet Festival and dropped it into the wastebasket.

A half hour later, outside the Actons Hotel, Jasper, in corduroy pants and brogues, and with a windbreaker over his sweater, slung his bags into the back of the Jaguar.

He drove north, up through Cobh and on through Youhal. By the time he reached Dungarvan on the N25, the sun had given way to clouds; in Waterford he turned onto the N9, broad and fast, and at Nass got onto the N7. In a pouring rain, he passed the turnoff that would have brought him, finally, to Ballynagh, but drove on. Twenty minutes later, he was on the N81 from western Wicklow into Dublin. Traffic was slowed by the rain, then stopped; there'd been a washout. Raincoated Gardai splashed along the roadside.

Jasper, arms resting on the steering wheel of the Jaguar, watched the windshield wiper click back and forth. Torrey. As always, the thought of Torrey brought a humorous twitch to his lips, not quite a smile. Torrey. Hopeless as a cook, a genetic marvel at languages, and as stubborn as Joan of Arc. Out of so simple an incident! She on her Peugeot, a nasty pair of young bullies on the road, and then Dakin, her rescuer. Out of that incident, Torrey would valiantly fight the equivalent of the War of the Roses.

In the gray rain, a flashlight was signaling. The cars ahead were beginning to move. Jasper inched the car forward, thinking: But, no. It wasn't that Torrey felt she owed Dakin something. It was about Dakin's belief in his mother's innocence. Torrey didn't *know* that Natalie Cameron hadn't killed Raphael Ricard. But if there was any chance that Dakin's mother was innocent, Ms. Torrey Tunet, the stubborn Ms. Tunet, was going to try to prove it. But she'd do it with sadness because, win or lose, what it was going to expose would break Dakin Cameron's heart. So, then.

"Move on, move on!" A garda in a yellow slicker waved his flashlight in an arc and the line of cars picked up speed.

The outskirts of Dublin, finally. He looked at his watch. Twenty past nine. He drove onto Clanbrassil Street, made a right at South Circular Road, then took the first left. He drove slowly down this unfamiliar, narrower street. Ah, there! A car was departing, leaving room to park. He tooled his way into the spot, shut off the motor, and said aloud, "For you, Torrey, my love, I've given up the Twenty-fourth International Gourmet Festival." Days of dining at the Kinsale Good Food Circle, the ten choicest restaurants in Ireland.

So what he was about to do had better pay off.

50

At nine-forty on Friday morning, Winifred Moore, seated at a window-side table in Finney's, crushed out her cigarette in the extra saucer beside her teacup. Through the window, she watched Sergeant Bryson carry folding chairs, four at a time, from Grogans' Needlework Shop to the Garda station directly across the street. He had already made two trips. In the window glass, she could see her reflection. She was wearing her favorite hat, the Australian outback hat with the chin strap. She and Sheila had breakfasted at eight o'clock at Castle Moore. Then she'd taken a half hour's invigorating walk to the bridle path and back, pedometer strapped to her ankle. Now this soul-satisfying, body-satisfying cup of hot tea. It was still twenty minutes before the informal meeting that had been so suddenly called by Inspector Egan O'Hare.

"What's it all *about*?" Sheila asked, poking at her empty teacup. She'd been fretful ever since yesterday when the call had come from Sergeant Bryson. She'd planned a morning of correspondence.

"If I were a betting woman, Sheila, I'd say it's something Torrey Tunet has a hand in."

"Winifred, that's an *incredibly* awkward sentence!"

Winifred, gazing from the window, said, "There's Natalie Cameron with Dakin. They're just going in. She's the most romantic-looking woman I've ever—And look, that blue BMW. What a careless way to park! It's Kate Burnside. Why's *she* here?"

At a few minutes to ten, Inspector Egan O'Hare, standing beside his desk, said "Good morning," and smiled at the expectant faces. Here they all were, or almost all. Among them, a murderer.

An informal meeting. "Be sure to say *informal*," he'd told Sergeant Bryson, giving him the list. He'd long since discovered that psychologically the word *informal* made the guilty lay down their guard. They translated it as "negligible." It wasn't official. It didn't count. It was safe. The guilty would feel they had a chance to spy, get the lay of the land. Yet each time in the past, the innocent-appearing informal meeting had trapped the guilty. What looked like honey was actually glue.

O'Hare glanced over at Ms. Torrey Tunet, who was standing at the back, beside the soda machine. She was wearing that bandanna around her dark hair, the turquoise scarf with the peacocks. Her talisman, he'd heard, something to do with her father, the Romanian. She had on a red jumper and jeans. Nelson, that opportunistic dog, sat beside her, as though on guard. Give him a biscuit and he was yours.

Ms. Tunet met O'Hare's gaze. And he thought, All right, then, Ms. Torrey Tunet, here we are. *Leave no stone unturned.* That was the motto of Chief Superintendent Emmet O'Reilly at Dublin Castle. O'Hare thought wryly: What good that a man feared neither God nor the devil, yet quailed before the cold-eyed assessment of Chief Superintendent Emmet O'Reilly, each word in his overly educated voice an icicle? He dared not risk it. Five minutes past ten.

"Oh, sorry! We're *sorry*!" The door had opened once again. "We're sorry! Marcy's bike had a flat." Willie Hern and Marcy McGann. A flurry. Sergeant Bryson unfolded two more chairs and set them down beside Brenda Plant, who nodded hello.

So that was it. All here. Inspector O'Hare's gaze took them in: Winifred Moore in a sort of cowboy-looking hat with a chin strap; beside her was her London friend, Sheila Flaxton, who was wrapped in a fuzzy beige shawl. In front of them sat Kate Burnside, whose dark hair was in two long braids though she was a woman in her midthirties. Still a beauty, despite the ravages of unchecked drinking and God knows what, there were unsavory rumors. She had shrugged off a brown shiny leather jacket and wore a peach-colored silk shirt open at the throat.

In front of Kate Burnside sat Natalie Cameron. O'Hare had the passing thought that her kind of beauty was indefinable. A broad brow, a blunt nose, the curve of a cheek; you could look a thousand times and never define the source of that unutterable beauty. She was in a black sweater and dove gray pants. Beside her was the boy, Dakin. Dark-haired, his mother's broad brow, a handsome, troubled face. For a change the boy wasn't wearing one of his yellow-brown jerseys but a suede jacket and navy shirt. On the folding chair beside Dakin sat Sean O'Boyle, freshly shaved, in a real suit. Next to him was Jessie Dugan, hands clasped in her lap and looking like an attentive schoolgirl. All here, Ms. Tunet.

It would be tricky. Standing before his desk, he managed a cryptic statement about exploring a possible connection between two recent violent events in Ballynagh, "both of which involved Canadians." He smiled at the mystified faces, though of course everyone knew that by "violence" in one of the cases, he meant "murder." He felt perspiration under his arms. So. The witnesses. He took a breath:

"Ms. Plant. If you don't mind."

"Oh, my!" Ms. Plant gave a startled laugh. Then with a shudder, she recounted her terrifying experience at the gates of Sylvester Hall. She wore a navy suit over a high-necked lavendar sweater, and with her short peroxided hair tamed and anchored above her ears by two curved little combs, she looked composed, though in the telling, she put a hand to her heart and her mascared blue eyes went wide. "Then, *jazz* music! And Ms. Tunet on her bicycle!"

Inspector O'Hare nodded. Marcy McGann was next. Marcy, in cherry-colored lipstick, said she hadn't seen a thing. "Not a thing," she mumbled, and cast a sidelong glance at Ms. Tunet. Neither had Willie Hern seen anything, "because of the curve in the road."

"Miss Tunet?" Torrey Tunet told the rest, right up to the arrival of the ambulance and the victim, Mr. Thomas Brannigan, taken off to Grasshill Hospital. So that was that. "I would've *died* of fright in Ms. Plant's shoes!" came Sheila Flaxton's whispered voice, followed by Winifred Moore's exasperated shushing.

But, curiously, Inspector O'Hare now smiled indulgently around at the attentive faces. "As you're probably aware, witnesses often are confused about what they've seen. Tests have shown a remarkable discrepancy between what actually happened and what a person *thinks* he saw happen. In this case, that appears to be so.

"Among the brambles at the gates where Mr. Brannigan was struck down, our investigation has turned up a bloodstained stone. The blood is Mr. Brannigan's blood type. So there you are! Ms. Plant saw *something* strike Mr. Brannigan. As for the rest, hysteria surely played a part." He smiled sympathetically at Ms. Plant.

"But—" Brenda Plant looked bewildered. "A *stone*? But I saw—You mean it wasn't a club, it was a *stone*? But I distinctly—Well, now I don't know!" She rubbed her forehead.

Someone's hoarse whisper: "Hallucinations, Sheila. The stuff of poetry!"

A rustling and shifting of feet while Inspector O'Hare leafed through a batch of papers he picked up from his desk. Willy Hern tiptoed quietly to the soda machine, but then there was a clank and the can rattled down. Marcy McGann stifled giggles until her pretty face turned almost as red as her hair.

"Now." Inspector O'Hare tapped a sheet of pale green paper and looked up. "Two Canadians attacked, one killed. Naturally, one presupposes a connection. I turn now to the results of forensic tests made concerning the murder of Raphael Ricard." His gaze came to rest on Katherine Burnside. "Miss Burnside. A few questions."

51

In the folding chair a few feet from O'Hare's desk, Katherine Burnside raised her brows in surprise. "Yes, Inspector O'Hare?" Amusement in her voice. She ran a hand over the back of the neck of her peach-colored silk shirt and pulled a thick braid forward to lie on her breast. Holding it, running her fingers absentmindedly along it, she gazed back at him. He drew a breath.

"Ms. Burnside, I have a report here from Dublin Castle. It concerns the killing of Mr. Raphael Ricard on Tuesday, October seventeenth. A penknife was the murder weapon. Forensic tests have revealed vestiges of various fingerprints on the knife. Yours among them."

Indrawn breaths from the listeners, someone gasped, then a waiting. Nelson snapped at a fly. In the silence, the snap of his teeth could be heard.

Inspector O'Hare did not take his eyes from Ms. Burnside's face. Her look was one of stunned disbelief. She said, "*My* fingerprints? I can't—That can't be, Inspector! Impossible!" And again, "Im*poss*ible."

"An error is always possible, Ms. Burnside," O'Hare said agreeably, "though we have a set of your fingerprints taken from—but that doesn't matter. Fingerprinting is a simple procedure. So if you object, and if you would submit your fingerprints to confirm the match of—"

"Never mind!" Kate Burnside's long and beautiful and paint-stained fingers twisted and twisted the black braid. She bit her full lower lip and stared at Inspector O'Hare. Then she shrugged. "Well?"

Inspector O'Hare, triumphant, suppressed a strong desire to again look over at Ms. Torrey Tunet. *My compliments, Ms. Tunet.* He said, "If you would care to explain, Ms. Burnside . . ."

"No, Inspector. I would not care to explain. But I hardly have an alternative . . . or am I wrong?" Even cornered, Kate Burnside was mocking him. Never mind.

"Quite right, Ms. Burnside." He folded his arms. "So if you please . . ." On his left, he was aware of Dakin Cameron swiping a hand through his dark hair. The wall clock ticked. Waiting, O'Hare had the impression that Kate Burnside had begun to hold on to that braid as though on to a life line.

"This is exactly what happened." Her throaty voice had a defensive loudness; no one in the room had to strain to hear her:

"I'm an old friend of Natalie Cameron's. I've known Dakin since he was a child. We remained friends, though his mother and I had drifted apart. Once in a while he'd confide in me. So . . ." A deep breath.

"A week ago Thursday, Dakin visited me. He told me that someone was blackmailing his mother, demanding that she deliver money to him at the cairn. And he said, 'She says she will never go to the cairn and give him money. But *for some reason* she refuses to report it to Inspector O'Hare."

Kate Burnside stopped. She looked back at O'Hare. "Dakin was worried that the blackmailer might retaliate by harming his mother. He was afraid for her. She was acting 'off somewhere,' as he put it—" Kate stopped.

Inspector O'Hare waited with a vague feeling that he was on a path through a wilderness. Kate Burnside sat gazing into space. A silence, a waiting.

Kate Burnside blinked as though coming back to herself. She said; "I wanted to help Natalie. We'd once been good friends. *Best* friends. And Dakin, so anxious, so worried! I didn't know how I could help, but I'd try. So that Saturday, in Natalie's stead, I went at noon to meet the blackmailer." She stopped.

Indrawn breaths; then the room was still. O'Hare, waiting, said at last, "And?"

"He was there, at the cairn. A man, a Canadian, I know the accent, I've Canadian cousins. I told him I was a friend of Natalie's and that she'd told me she'd no idea what secret she could possibly be hiding, that there was nothing she might be guilty of. Nothing about which to pay blackmail. It was all nonsense. She would never come to the cairn to pay blackmail. Never! He didn't believe me. He was angry, impatient. But then he laughed. 'I'll write her again,' he told me, 'a letter that will bring her. Tuesday noon. She knows why I'm here. Otherwise, she'd have called the Gardai. So she'll come.'

"I didn't know what else to do, how to help. But all Tuesday morning, while I was working on a painting, I felt drawn to the cairn to see for certain. I could see myself going to the cairn and saying to that blackmailer, 'You see? You'll get no money from Natalie. She'll never come! Let her alone!' And I'd even lie, and say, 'I believe Natalie has already informed the Gardai.'

"So I went, I couldn't help it. But when I got to the cairn, he was lying there. The blood! My foot touched something. I picked it up. It was a penknife. At once I flung it away. And I thought, *Natalie has come after all.*"

―――――

Indrawn breaths. Appalled faces turned to look at Natalie Cameron, who sat immobile. Sheila Flaxton made a mewling sound. Winifred Moore lit a cigarette with an unsteady hand, then at a reproving sign from Sergeant Bryson, crushed it out under her boot.

Inspector O'Hare said, "That's how your fingerprints got on the penknife, Ms. Burnside?"

"That's exactly how, Inspector."

"And then, Ms. Burnside? What did you do then?"

Kate Burnside said, "What? Then? Oh, then I ran from there! I was so—But when I got back to my studio—it's in that old O'Sullivan's barn—I thought, maybe Natalie had gone to the cairn without bringing the blackmail money. So he'd lost his head and attacked her! Maybe *in defending herself from him*, she—" Ms. Burnside put a hand to her throat. "So I ran back to the cairn to take the penknife away. To save her.

"But when I got back, coming out of the woods I saw several people standing over there beyond the meadow, at the cairn. You, Inspector, Sergeant Bryson. Others. I was too late."

52

Inspector O'Hare, after a moment, nodded. "Thank you, Ms. Burnside." He glanced from under his brows at Natalie Cameron. She was regarding her childhood friend with the incredulity of someone seeing a swan flying over the moon. Beside her, Dakin had flashed a startled glance at Kate Burnside, then away. As for Kate Burnside herself, she shot a challenging look around, as though daring anyone not to believe her.

Inspector O'Hare' waited until Kate Burnside, chin out-thrust, looked back at him. Then, "So, Ms. Burnside, because of a childhood friendship, nothing more, you did what you could to help Natalie Cameron." He frowned. "However, your fingerprints on the knife have muddied the—have created a complication. It is now not entirely clear that Natalie Cameron was the one who, with the penknife—"

"*What?*" Kate Burnside's voice was incredulous. "You can't possibly mean, Inspector—But I'd have no *reason* to kill him! The man was a stranger to me!" Her paint-stained fingers clutched at the collar of her shirt. She gave a wild little laugh, "Oh, Christ! I *have* got myself in a mess!" Dazed, Kate Burnside sank back in her chair.

Inspector O'Hare himself felt a bit of a shiver. Nothing involving the murder of Mr. Ricard was as it seemed. Fingerprints on the knife, other fingerprints besides Natalie Cameron's, a nightmare of fingerprints. Get on with it, approach with caution, there are snakes in the box.

O'Hare, with a sudden qualm, refrained from looking at Ms. Torrey Tunet standing back there with Nelson by the soda machine. Go along? Back out? Natalie Cameron had gone to the cairn, after all, to meet the blackmailer. But instead of bringing the blackmail money, she *could* have rushed out of Sylvester Hall with the penknife and a frightened, furious intent to kill. Seen departing Sylvester Hall in such a state — or otherwise?

Inspector O'Hare looked over at Jessie Dugan, who was sitting beside Sean O'Boyle. "Jessie, if you don't mind."

Jessie didn't at all mind. She was, in fact, thrilled. She'd have tons to tell Hannah at Castle Moore after, her in her new jacket, and she'd washed her hair last night and it had come out just right, the little wisps around her cheeks curling up in spite of the dry weather.

"Jessie," Inspector O'Hare said, "would you tell us exactly what happened that Tuesday morning at Sylvester Hall? As nearly as you can remember."

"Yes, sir." Jessie felt comfortable with Inspector O'Hare; she'd known him all her life and her mother had almost married him when she was a slip of a girl, so the story went, which meant he could almost have been her father. It made a bond.

She said, "First thing that morning, a letter came in the post. It didn't have a stamp. Someone had just stuck it in our postbox at the end of the avenue. It was the third letter to come like that in the last two weeks. The third! Just *put* there. Scary, somehow. Like I said to Mr. O'Boyle; he was working in the greenhouse that morning. 'A *third* letter', I told him."

Jessie looked over at Sean O'Boyle. He looked so different, clean-shaven, and in the brown jacket and clean white shirt, not in his usual greasy sweater. His sister, Caitlin, probably had made him shave and had ironed the shirt. He was always babying some plant or other, like whatever greens in that flower pot on his knees. She looked back at Inspector O'Hare:

"Mr. O'Boyle said I was too jumpy. He said it was from seeing too many scary television movies. Grisly stuff and all. But I don't know.

"Anyway, Ms. Cameron had gone out early to Dunlavin, to some meeting. Low-cost housing. So she didn't get to read the letter until she got back, almost noon. She must've read it soon's she came in the door. I'd put the morning's mail in the tray on the table in the front hall."

" 'Must've,' Jessie?"

"Well, I heard her cry out. It was an awful sound! Like something you'd read about in a book."

A silence, then a delighted whisper, Winifred Moore's voice. "I know *exactly*. Sheila, this young woman's a poet!"

O'Hare said, louder than usual, in a reprimand to Winifred Moore, "And then, Jessie?"

"I came from the kitchen right away. It'd frightened me, her crying out like that. I asked if something was the matter but she said no, and ran right past me up the stairs. Before I could turn around she was back down and I asked her about raspberries for lunch, but she went right past me saying eggs would do, and she was out the door and down the steps. The dogs, Crackers and Buster, were whining and running back and forth in the hall instead of Ms. Cameron taking them out with her as she'd ordinarily have done."

"And when Ms. Cameron returned? When was that?"

Jessie shook her head. "I don't know. Breda would've made omelettes if she'd come. I was doing the rooms and like that. Breda and I had a bit of lunch, waiting. Sean O'Boyle said—But I don't know. I didn't see her. Next we knew was when we heard about . . . about *it*."

O'Hare nodded. Three letters. He slanted a glance at Ms. Torrey Tunet back there, leaning against the soda machine. Three letters. Just as she'd said. Pedaling around on her bicycle, that turquoise bandana with figures of peacocks around her head, and plucking clues off thistles and furze, far as he could tell. He felt a stir of envy and exasperation.

"Thank you, Jessie." He turned to Sean O'Boyle, who was sitting next to Jessie Dugan. The wall clock struck half eleven. Nelson barked for his usual biscuit; O'Hare waited patiently until Sergeant Bryson opened the box of biscuits and gave a biscuit to Nelson, who otherwise would have carried on.

"Mr. O'Boyle, you were aware of all three unstamped letters that Jessie Dugan spoke of?"

Sean O'Boyle nodded. "Yes. Never happened before. In the old days, Ms. Sybil's time, I used to be the one to go down the avenue for the post. Never saw such a thing as unstamped mail. Course, t'was a pittance for a stamp in those days."

O'Hare nodded. "And on that Tuesday?"

"I was busy in the greenhouse, so I didn't see Ms. Cameron return from Dunlavin. And I didn't see her leave Sylvester Hall either time."

O'Hare caught him up. "Either time, Mr. O'Boyle?"

Sean O'Boyle looked confused. "I mean, I didn't get to Sylvester Hall early enough to see Ms. Cameron go off to her meeting in Dunlavin. Later, being in the greenhouse, I didn't see her go off before lunch. If that's what you mean?"

"Yes," O'Hare said, "that's what I meant."

187

But now, as though Sean O'Boyle had become a shadow, O'Hare took a breath and his gaze rested on Ms. Torrey Tunet; he was getting that feeling of anticipation, because now they'd be breaking open the shell and getting to the nut of it. Ms. Tunet, though, gave no sign. She looked her usual exasperating self, standing there watching him, meanwhile fondling one of Nelson's floppy ears. Momentarily O'Hare saw her again in the red slicker, leaning forward on the edge of the chair next to his desk Wednesday afternoon; he was hearing her impassioned voice. And now, as then, he had a prickly feeling at the back of his neck as her incredible tale unfolded. Then, confirmation from Dublin Castle's forensics. So that now —

From down Butler Street, St. Andrew's clock boomed the noontime hour, the smell of frying sausage drifted from somewhere, Nelson barked, Sheila Flaxton could be heard whispering to Winifred Moore that the folding chair was making her back ache. Sergeant Bryson was holding up his wrist and tapping his wristwatch significantly, as though the racket of St. Andrew's clock had somehow escaped the notice of his superior.

O'Hare said, "I think a recess is in order."

53

They were all back within the hour, only minutes after Inspector O'Hare had swallowed Finney's Friday Special, the fried fish sandwich that Sergeant Bryson brought him. For himself, Bryson had the vegetable salad, no dressing. "Nutritious," Bryson had said, a bit on the gloomy side. He'd made their tea on the electric two-burner on the table beside his desk.

Inspector O'Hare saw that Ms. Tunet was standing against the wall beside the first row of chairs, thumbs hooked in the pockets of her jeans. Despite her red jumper and jeans, she looked oddly exotic, it was that turquoise bandanna with the peacocks.

O'Hare leaned back against his desk, crossing his ankles. A light scent of perfume reached him, it came from Natalie Cameron, settling into her place in the first row, barely a few feet from where he stood. Her face had a wide-awake look, alert, her hazel eyes more curious than fearful. A *waiting* face, thought O'Hare. Her son Dakin, though, conveyed something else. Chin out a bit. Braced. A boy Stoic, an interior fox gnawing.

O'Hare cleared his throat. "Pursuing a possible connection between the murder of Mr. Ricard and the attack on Mr.

Brannigan," and he turned toward Ms. Tunet. "Ms. Tunet, in my investigation I learned that you visited Mr. Brannigan at Grasshill Hospital. Exactly why, Ms. Tunet?"

Ms. Tunet looked astonished. Her gray eyes went wide. "After all! I practically saved Mr. Brannigan's life! Running to the Hall for help! Getting you and Sergeant Bryson! He might've died! All that."

And because you're so damned nosy, Inspector O'Hare refrained from saying.

"His head was bandaged," Ms. Tunet went on. "He was weak. He appreciated my visit. He wasn't exactly coherent. But he struggled to talk. He mentioned the name Ricard." Ms. Tunet gazed off in memory. "He told me of a frightening connection between himself and Raphael Ricard."

Intakes of breath. There it was: incontrovertibly a link between the brutal attack and the murder. Both horrors, incredibly, right here in Ballynagh, this peaceful village lying in the valley among the mountains on whose sides sheep peacefully grazed, and if it weren't for the fishing in the streams down from those mountains, not a dozen visitors a year would have supported the five-room Nolan's Bed and Breakfast, full Irish breakfast notwithstanding. And only sixteen pounds a night, single or double.

Torrey tried not to look at Natalie Cameron. But from under her eyelids she saw Natalie reach out and put a hand on Dakin's arm; in response, he put his own hand over hers. A nervous cough from Sean O'Boyle on Dakin's left. Beside where Torrey stood, Kate Burnside on the folding chair crossed her legs; she was wearing stockings. Torrey smelled cigarette smoke. Winifred Moore again, but Sergeant Bryson would take care of that.

"A connection, Ms. Tunet?"

Torrey hesitated, hating where this investigation would

have to go, hated that the shell would have to be cracked open, all revealed. But there was no other way; she'd known it on Wednesday afternoon when she'd come to Inspector O'Hare and laid the things on his desk. *No other way*. A pity for Natalie Cameron over there on the folding chair; in Florence, in the Uffizi Gallery, the Michelangelo, the down-turned head with its broad forehead, the curve of the eyelid: in this version, wearing a black sweater and dove gray pants.

"Ms. Tunet?"

She took a breath. "Mr. Brannigan told me that he had followed Mr. Ricard to Ireland to kill him."

From the listeners, gasps. Torrey, barely a dozen feet from Inspector O'Hare, could see tension tighten the muscles in his face.

"A disturbing confidence for Mr. Brannigan to divulge to you, Ms. Tunet." O'Hare's voice was sympathetic. "It as good as involved *you*."

"Yes." *Damned right*.

"To kill Mr. Ricard. Exactly why, Ms. Tunet?"

"He didn't tell me." Lying, Torrey met Inspector O'Hare's keen eyes under the gray-white brows. What Brannigan had revealed to her wouldn't help Natalie. No, she'd have to go down that other road. She felt again the little shiver when in the cottage, staring at the bloodstained stone on Jasper's handkerchief on the kitchen table, the thought had come to her . . . supposing . . .

"Ms. Tunet?" Inspector O'Hare's voice was bland, patient. Ah, yes, of course. That other road. He knew her lying had been for the listeners. Or rather, for one single listener among those seated on the folding chairs.

She said, "It occurred to me, Inspector, that the attack on Tom Brannigan had prevented him from killing Raphael Ricard."

The word "killing" was a hard little pebble dropping into the silence.

O'Hare folded his arms. "Are you suggesting, Ms. Tunet, that *that* had been its purpose?"

"Yes, Inspector. Mr. Brannigan was struck down to stop him from killing Mr. Ricard."

That hard little pebble again dropped into a silence that was immediately broken:

"Oh, my! Winifred, I feel absolutely *faint*!"

"Sheila," Winifred Moore sounded merely annoyed, "you have the constitution of an ox. Just sit up straight and let a little air get into your lungs. Or leave. Wait outside in the Jeep." But Sheila Flaxton merely put a hand to her breastbone and pulled her fuzzy shawl more closely around her shoulders. Marcy McGann giggled.

"*Then*," Torrey said, "last Friday I had occasion to visit Nolan's Bed and Breakfast. I wanted to . . . to ask Sara Hobbs what she charges on weekends, I'm expecting a guest or two later on, and the cottage is too small." She drew a breath. "Anyway, Friday. Ms. Plant was sitting in the reception room waiting for Sergeant Bryson, they were going antiquing. Meanwhile, she was doodling with a pencil on an ad in *Body Beautiful* magazine. Sergeant Bryson arrived a couple of minutes later. After they'd left, I picked up the magazine; I was waiting for Sara Hobbs, who'd gone down for the post."

"What's she *getting* at?" Sheila Flaxton's whisper to Winifred Moore brought a sharp glance from Inspector O'Hare.

Torrey said, "I saw then that Ms. Plant hadn't been *doodling* on the ad. She'd been *editing* it."

The silence of curiosity; it was as though a strange bird had suddenly flown into the garda station.

"The ad was for the Roslina exercise method. I remembered that in America, when I was growing up, there was a popular television series, *Roslina, the Warrior Maiden*. Shlock, but fun: the warrior maiden with gold armbands, breast plates and loincloth, wielding a long, snaky whip, leaping over rocks, splattering her enemies right and left. The series starred Brenda Roslina, a Polish exercise champion who had emigrated to America."

Torrey stopped. She looked at Brenda Plant. "I'm an interpreter, that's my business. So I know languages. For instance, Polish. *Roslina* means 'plant.'"

Intakes of breath. In the second row, Brenda Plant was a beautifully coifed block of wood with eyes of blue glass.

Torrey went on, "That made me curious enough to call the City of Cork. I learned there is no Irish antiques show scheduled." She couldn't refrain from casting a sympathetic glance at Sergeant Jimmy Bryson's face. Astonishment? Disbelief? She continued.

"It seemed ridiculous, but it occurred to me that Ms. Plant *herself* might have struck down Tom Brannigan. No great feat for the ex–Warrior Maiden to, say, throw a stone a bare few feet across the road and strike him down."

The block of wood that was Brenda Plant sat immovable, blue eyes staring at Torrey Tunet.

Inspector O'Hare said, "Ms. Plant?"

54

Ms. Plant?" Inspector O'Hare waited.

Brenda Plant tucked back a strand of blond hair with a firm hand. She looked from Inspector O'Hare to Ms. Torrey Tunet:

"That is the wildest, most in*sane*—!" Her voice was contemptuous. "It doesn't even warrant an answer. Plant! Roslina! Presupposing, Ms. Tunet, that I'm some kind of obsessed psychotic who goes about snapping whips and hurling rocks!" Furious blue eyes. "As for the antiques show in Cork—I have my own private reasons for wishing to visit Cork! It was not necessary for me to divulge them to Inspector O'Hare simply because I happened to witness that *horrifying* attack on Mr. Brannigan." Brenda Plant glared at Ms. Tunet. "*My* business is *my* business, Ms. Tunet!"

Silence, astonishment; then a snort of approval from Sergeant Bryson, who turned an indignant look on Ms. Tunet. Winifred Moore took advantage of Sergeant Bryson's emotional involvement to light another cigarette. Sean O'Boyle gazed pensively at Sergeant Bryson's handsome, flushed face. Inspector O'Hare saw that Natalie Cameron and Dakin were as bewildered as though it had begun to snow inside the Garda station. As for himself, he had a feel-

194

ing of being on a train that had gone off the rails. He said, "Thank you, Ms. Plant."

Ms. Plant said, "Well, really!" She twisted a ruby ring on her finger and gave Ms. Tunet a furious look. Kate Burnside laughed, a hysterical little laugh. The phone on Sergeant Bryson's desk buzzed. Bryson picked it up. "The what? *Evening Standard?* No, nothing further. Inspector O'Hare is in . . . in Galway. Yes, Thursday, as scheduled. In Dublin. The son involved? No further information on that score. Yes, back tomorrow." He hung up and refrained from looking toward Ms. Cameron and her son. Winifred Moore's whisper to Sheila was loud: "The *Standard!* That dirty rag! Madame La Farge at the guillotine!" From Ms. Tunet a soft whistle of "The Lion Sleeps Tonight," and then, "Inspector? May I continue?"

"In a moment, Ms. Tunet." O'Hare turned to the desk behind him and fumbled up some sheets of paper to cover a momentary panic. Had he let the impassioned Ms. Tunet lead him down a garden path where he'd be squashed like a bug? Then he steadied. This was, after all an *informal* meeting. It need never be exposed to the press. Besides, he was in it now; no way to back out. He frowned down at the papers he held, pretending a need to study them further, his heart beginning to beat more normally. In a minute he'd be ready to proceed. He was grateful, though, that Sheila Flaxton now got up and hurried into the toilet; and then it appeared that Marcy McGann had the same need. She emerged with her red-orange hair recombed and her cherry red lipstick renewed, and settled down beside Willy Hern.

Inspector O'Hare put the papers down on his desk. He nodded to Ms. Tunet. "Yes, Ms. Tunet. Please continue." He wondered how she could stand so at ease, thumbs hooked into her jeans pockets; but then he saw the faint dew of perspiration on her brow.

Torrey drew a breath. "You know how something can tease your mind? I remembered that at Grasshill Hospital, Mr. Brannigan had told me that, half out of his head, he'd left a message on Mr. Ricard's recording machine in Montreal saying, "I'm going to kill you." And I began to wonder: had anyone known that Tom Brannigan had gone rushing off to Ireland to kill Mr. Ricard?

"So I looked up a listing of Montreal detective agencies on the Internet and called one of them. The Dirkson Agency." She stopped. She was back in the cottage staring at the bloodstained stone on the table, she was getting up and at the kitchen sink drinking a glass of cold water, then crossing to her desk and making the phone calls that had cost her four hundred dollars because she wanted the information within hours.

"Ms. Tunet?"

"Oh, sorry!" She felt chilled; it had darkened a bit in the station, the sky outside having clouded over. "I wondered if Mr. Ricard had a lover who visited him, maybe had a key to his apartment. So—"

"So—" O'Hare couldn't resist. "So after Ricard had left for Ireland, the lover, say, might've found Mr. Brannigan's message on Mr. Ricard's answering machine?"

"Absolutely, Inspector. That occurred to me. That whoever it was could've found the message. I guessed that that person could've recognized the touch of brogue in the caller's voice and suspected it was Tom Brannigan, who owned The Citadel Bookshop and whom Rafe Ricard was courting as a client."

"Must have?"

Torrey nodded. "Well, it was a guess. So I called The

Citadel Bookshop, and found out that just after Tom Brannigan had left for Ireland, a woman had called wanting urgently to speak to him. The clerk told her he had left for Ireland. That, of course, was all she really wanted to know."

Torrey stopped; she drew a breath. "The clerk said the woman had been excited and that hanging up she'd muttered a hasty good-bye, 'only it wasn't *"good-bye"*.' The clerk tried to imitate it for me, and said, 'It was like the Russian word for good-bye, *do zvidaniya*, but not quite.' So of course I knew."

"Knew?"

"Well, of course, yes! Of the twenty-six most common languages, the word *good-bye* is similar in only two: Russian and Polish. The Polish is *do widzenia*."

So quiet. A waiting. Torrey said, "I called the Dirkson Agency again. They found out for me that, yes, Ms. Brenda Plant had booked an Aer Lingus flight from Montreal to Dublin leaving that same night."

55

Brenda Plant sat staring at Torrey Tunet. "*You!* What did it have to do with *you*? Nosing about! What's it *your* business? Of course I rushed off to Ireland to warn Mr. Ricard! Tom Brannigan was out of his mind! He was murderous." Her voice was uneven. She breathed quickly and patted her chest, calming herself. She turned to Inspector O'Hare. She spoke directly to him, as though the two of them were alone, perhaps in comfortable chairs somewhere before a fireplace with a crackling fire, not in this Garda station.

"Inspector, you'll understand, when I explain." She took a breath. "I'd arrived in Montreal from Buffalo to spend a weekend with Mr. Ricard. I knew he'd gone to Ireland on some business and expected to be back by then. But instead, I found that frightening message on his answering machine." She shuddered. "You can imagine! I was desperate to warn him, so I followed. You see?"

O'Hare nodded. "Of course. I quite—"

"Yes, of course, Inspector! In Ballynagh, I found there was only one bed and breakfast. Sara Hobbs was at the desk in the reception room at the top of the stairs. When I registered, I saw on the register that Mr. Ricard was there, but that Tom Brannigan hadn't yet arrived—somehow I'd gotten there ahead of him. A tremendous relief! Later I found out he'd had car trouble on the road."

O'Hare nodded. The car that Tom Brannigan had rented at the airport was still at Duffy's garage. Duffy had mentioned engine trouble on the way to Ballynagh. Sergeant Jimmy Bryson had made a notation of that at the time of the attack on Brannigan.

Brenda Plant sat forward, her face pale, her light blue eyes looking into the past. "Right away, I called Mr. Ricard's room. But there was no answer. So I sat there in the reception room, waiting for him to show up.

"But instead, Tom Brannigan arrived. His face was a horror: white, tight, *lethal*. I held up a newspaper before me in case he looked my way. Sara Hobbs chatted away to him while he registered, but he barely said a word. He called Mr. Ricard's room from the desk and got no answer.

"So he rushed right back down the stairs. I followed. I was afraid to leave him in case he found Rafe. He went into a pub down the street. O'Malley's. I thought, what if he has a gun? What if Rafe was in the pub and I'd hear gun shots? What if—"

O'Hare started as the phone on Sergeant Bryson's desk buzzed. And buzzed. Brenda Plant waited. Sergeant Bryson made no move to the phone. He was a statue, his gaze fixed incredulously on Brenda Plant. Inspector O'Hare went to Bryson's desk, lifted the receiver an inch, then placed it back in its cradle. "Go on, Ms. Plant."

Brenda Plant smoothed her blond hair with a nervous gesture. "Well . . . after a few minutes Tom Brannigan came out of the pub. He was walking like a . . . a wooden man. I followed him up the street and across a little bridge. On the road, I mingled with some women returning home from some sort of jumble sale. Gradually they dropped off, going up paths or side roads. Finally there was just Tom Brannigan ahead. He stopped outside tall, wrought-iron gates. He just stood there. Only trees and bushes and silence all around; and along the sides of the road, bits of brush. And stones. And I thought, *Stop him now!*

"So I picked up a stone."

Inspector O'Hare refrained from looking at Ms. Tunet. From Marcy McGann he heard a whisper, presumably to Willie Hern, "It *wasn't* a blue jay!"

O'Hare said drily, "You covered yourself well, Ms. Plant. Screaming out to Ms. Tunet for help. Rushing to her on her bicycle."

Brenda Plant shrugged. "What else was I to do? I heard jazz, "Mack the Knife," so sudden, so *near!* I thought she might have glimpsed—or *they* might have," and she nodded toward Marcy McGann and Willie Hern. "I had to try."

O'Hare almost winced. He thought wryly of the seemingly terrified Ms. Plant in her olive green coat telling him of seeing a man smashing a club down on Brannigan's head.

Peripherally, he was aware, on his left, of a sudden movement as Dakin Cameron stood up, only to have his mother swiftly reach out and grasp his arm, shaking her head and pulling him back down. O'Hare shot a swift look at Ms. Tunet and saw at once that she too had seen the byplay; he was startled to discover how well he could read that young woman in her peacock bandanna. She was simply looking at him but she might just as well have said, *Do go on, Inspector.* The garda station was, after all, his arena. His confidence flowed back. He glanced with a touch of amusement at Sergeant Jimmy Bryson, who appeared dazed. He said, "Thank you, Ms. Plant."

Excited whispers, a general murmur; Inspector O'Hare

caught a "So *horr*ifying!" in a trembly voice from Sheila Fax-
ton, and from Willie Hern, an awed . . . and perhaps envious
"with a bloody *stone!*"

O'Hare rubbed his chin, waiting until the murmurs died
down. Then he looked over at Kate Burnside sitting with her
dark head tipped down, gazing blank-eyed before her. "Ms.
Burnside."

Kate Burnside looked up. Her brown eyes were heavy, her
face brooding and wretched. One hand had worried the top
button of her peach-colored silk shirt, so that the button now
hung loose.

"Yes, Inspector?" No mockery now. O'Hare felt a stir of
pity. No wonder apprehension rode Ms. Kate Burnside! Her
fingerprints were on the penknife.

"Ms. Burnside, if you don't mind. To go back a bit:
Your . . . ah, tale . . . You said that Mr. Ricard was attempting to blackmail Natalie Cameron."

"Yes. That's what I said, Inspector. For what it's worth."
Bitter, as though to say, *Stop plaguing me.*

"Thank you, Ms. Burnside." O'Hare had a familiar sense
of closing in; it was like the games of his childhood, hiding,
running, searching, the shouts of discovery, the culprit
sprawling, revealed. He turned to Brenda Plant.

"Ms. Plant, you stopped Mr. Brannigan from killing Mr.
Ricard. Did you know *why* Mr. Brannigan wanted to kill Mr.
Ricard?"

"Naturally not. I had no idea."

"I see." He was sweating under his arms again. *This is the
only way*, Ms. Tunet had said. No, not said: *begged*. As if it
were her own life she was begging for. Ms. Tunet, over there,
so innocent-looking, hands in the pockets of her jeans. Ms.
Tunet having once again proved herself a thief, and expecting

him to do more than turn a blind eye. And him, conniving. He reached behind him to his desk and picked up the wrinkled sheet of notepad paper with the note scrawled in a bold hand. "This," he said, and he read aloud: "People with guilty secrets are fair game. The bitch's secret is ugly enough to be worth twenty thousand pounds. More, if she balks. Back by Friday. R.' "

Brenda Plant cried out, an inarticulate cry. Then, "How did you get that? Sara Hobbs poking about among my things? Fat little snooping pig! Running to you with—That's illegal! This whole—this *village*. Conniving! It should be reported to police headquarters in Dublin." Indignant, fist to her chest, breathing hard, she said angrily, "All *right*! I knew about the blackmail. It's true, what Rafe said! Fair game! He was having financial problems and all of a sudden he found out about Natalie Cameron. Her rotten secret! He'd found out what she was: lily white on top, a lying, sleeping-around tramp underneath.

"So she killed him! *Killed* him, rather than give him the money! *Killed* him to keep her secret."

A crack of thunder, the sudden pound of rain against the plate glass. Inspector O'Hare looked over at Natalie Cameron beside Dakin. Her hazel eyes were wide, a waiting look; her lower lip caught between her teeth. O'Hare thought of the time he'd had the broken arm and while Dr. Collins was setting it, he'd bitten his lower lip until it bled all down his shirt. Now all those who belonged at Sylvester Hall would bleed.

Brenda Plant said, "Rafe knew about Natalie and the chauffeur back then, years back, at Sylvester Hall. Tom Brannigan, the chauffeur! Rafe knew that Dakin Cameron is Tom Brannigan's child."

———

Torrey hardly heard the gasps, the creaking of the folding chairs as the listeners leaned and stretched to glimpse at least Natalie Cameron's face or profile, or stared in shock at Dakin Cameron, who sat with one leg crossed over the other, an arm resting along the back of his mother's chair. *Good for you,* Torrey thought: Natalie and Dakin sitting there looking no more than slightly dazed. Prepared, thank God! At least that. Prepared in the library at Sylvester Hall yesterday morning, she telling Natalie Cameron what she'd discovered. Then Dakin called in from the coach house. She had stood at the library window looking out at Sean O'Boyle trimming the rhododenrons while off on a sofa near the fireplace Natalie had told Dakin who his father was. "It's the only way," Torrey had unhappily warned them before she left Sylvester Hall. Dakin had surprised her. At first, a stunned face; nothing more. Later, he had reached out and touched the unicorn bracelet on his mother's wrist. Then a shake of his head and a sigh. Torrey had noticed that the blue bruise had almost faded from his cheekbone.

In the Garda station, again a crack of thunder, the spatter of rain against the window; and now Brenda Plant saying, "Rafe told me, 'I'll just ask that hypocritical bitch, "How d'you think your son will feel if I tell him that his real father is the former chauffeur at Sylvester Hall? You sleeping with the chauffeur, then marrying Andrew Cameron to hide that you were pregnant by him. And palming off the baby to Andrew Cameron as his! But a DNA test can prove otherwise." ' "

Brenda Plant glanced scornfully over at Natalie Cameron. "Rafe said it was in the *Irish Times*, in the society news, that Natalie Cameron was about to marry again. 'She'll be frantic to pay me off!' he told me." Brenda Plant looked back at Inspector O'Hare. "But Natalie Cameron didn't pay. She killed."

Torrey for an instant closed her eyes. Brenda Plant had just showed why Natalie would have had good reason to rush furiously at Ricard with the penknife. Torrey shivered. It was a risk she'd had to take. And Natalie Cameron had trusted her. Chestnuts in the fire.

56

Inspector O'Hare's mouth was dry. He had a box of mixed fruit drops in his top desk drawer, but this was hardly the time. He mustn't lose the chain; no, it wasn't a chain, it was barely more than a thread. "Ms. Plant. Both you and Mr. Ricard were staying at Nolan's Bed and Breakfast, so you were in close contact, and—"

"No! Not at all! Barely a good-morning, what with Sara Hobbs so solicitous! Acting like a guard dog, protecting me from who knew what. The man with the club, I suppose. And Sergeant Bryson, on my heels every minute. So Rafe thought, *Risky. Better not.* Not even to talk to each other. Breakfast at separate tables."

"I see." Inspector O'Hare licked dry lips and longed to soothe his throat. But now he was inching along the thread. "Yet you and Mr. Ricard managed to meet secretly, away from Nolan's, despite the diffculty of your sprained ankle."

"I don't exactly follow?" Brenda Plant looked puzzled.

"You were seen meeting with Mr. Ricard near the cairn, in the west field near Castle Moore. More than once." The thread was getting taut. "It is only logical, from a police point of view, that you were conferring about the progress of—"

"That's an outrageous assumption!" Ms. Plant's face was furious. "Is this a trick? Trying to implicate me in the blackmail at the cairn! I never went there! I had nothing to do with the blackmail! I tried to dissuade Rafe from it entirely! I—"

"No, no! Ms. Plant! I don't mean to implicate you. Not at all!" O'Hare felt warm dampness under his arms. "Simply, it's police procedure to follow every—not to overlook anything. Likely it was only the need . . . the need for privacy between two lovers. So, in the fields . . ." O'Hare coughed. "It was only natural. Lovers. It was just that, since someone happened to witness—" He stopped. To his own amazement he felt a blush rising, heating his face.

"Witness?" Brenda Plant laughed. "What nonsense! There was nothing to witness. They're lying." She half turned and swept a glance over the listeners. She turned back to Inspector O'Hare. "What witness? Which of them? Who's the liar?"

"No one here. It was a child."

"A *child?*" Brenda Plant laughed again. "A boy? A girl? A child who made it up! Children do that. Wanting attention. Starting trouble. The witches of Salem. Burned at the stake. Tied up and drowned because of children's lies."

But from one of the listeners, a half laugh and a husky voice said, "It wasn't a lie. It did happen. Making love in the field."

57

Kate Burnside's voice. Chin tipped up, she turned to Inspector O'Hare. Her eyes were bright, there was mockery in her voice, color in her cheeks. She'd come alive again in these last minutes, a wilting plant that had been watered and now sprouted glossy green leaves and dewy blossoms. She said, "Oh, yes, Inspector! There was lovemaking in the fields! Lovemaking with the blackmailer. Only the woman wasn't Ms. Plant. It was Kate Burnside."

O'Hare waited. It was one thing he had learned to do early in his career, one of the most important. Kate Burnside was smiling, looking back at him as though challenging him. "Does that shock you, Inspector? Disgust you? Nettles on my back! Even that Saturday! Later, I brought wine. Wine, and October sun and his jacket under me. Each day, to meet him. Sunday! And Monday! Each day! I couldn't wait!" She gave a sudden, wild, shaky laugh. "Even one night at O'Sullivan's barn, where I paint! Even there!"

Inspector O'Hare felt buffeted. Struck. He had an astonishing sudden vision of young horses running free across the hills and valleys of Ireland. Nothing to do with the ruined, still-young face of Ms. Kate Burnside. Yet . . .

"You're lying!" Brenda Plant's voice was furious. Her face was pale. "He wouldn't! Rafe wouldn't! Never!"

Kate Burnside laughed. "Oh, please! You're a woman, after all. You were his lover. How could you not guess that *something*—A man like that!"

"Guess? Why would I?" Brenda Plant's voice was furious. "Do you suppose I'm clairvoyant? Do you think I'm Madame Something-or-other with a pack of cards? Or that I looked in a crystal ball and saw you and Rafe making love among the nettles or in a barn? Ridiculous! Of course I knew nothing of what you're talking about!"

A silence. Then from the back, near the soda machine, a new voice: "But Brenda! Ms. Plant! You *did* know."

58

Heads turned. Sergeant Jimmy Bryson, looking appalled at his own words, was staring at Ms. Brenda Plant. Inspector O'Hare, startled, shot a quick glance at Torrey Tunet, standing there with her thumbs hooked in the pockets of her jeans. She met his glance and raised an eyebrow.

O'Hare said, "Sergeant Bryson?"

But it was to Brenda Plant that Bryson spoke. "The tiddly old fellow, Danny. In Finney's, that Monday night, singing 'Reilly's Daughter' at the bar, then talking about the visiting chap with the suede fishing hat, how he'd fished for a bit of cuddly and caught himself a lulu. How Billy had spied them going into the O'Sullivan's barn one time. That's when you knew, isn't it." It was not a question. It was Sergeant Bryson bleakly confirming something to himself.

Brenda Plant said softly, mechanically, as though she were having a conversation with someone invisible, "Oh, *that* was bitter! After I'd almost killed Tom Brannigan to protect him! Then I hated him. *Hated* him!" She drew in a breath that caught on a sob. She put a hand to her throat.

Inspector O'Hare thought, *Now,* and he gave a little shudder as he felt something like a bead of quicksilver slide down his back between his shoulder blades; and it was almost as though he were hearing someone else say the comforting

209

words, but of course it was his voice and he was smiling sympathetically at Ms. Brenda Plant as he said, "Don't worry, Ms. Plant. Easy enough to prove you had no hand in the killing. We can quickly clear you of any involvement, any suggestion that you acted violently when you discovered— That's easily done. We can simply take your fingerprints to compare to the unidentified—"

"*No!*" An involuntary cry of panic. Brenda Plant's hands flew up as though warding off a blow. "No! No, no!" Her eyes met Inspector O'Hare's keen gaze. A long look passed between them; it was fully a half minute before Brenda Plant sank back and dropped her upraised hands to her lap.

Dead silence. Then "My God!" Winifred Moore's strong voice carried. "The Warrior Woman killed him! With that puny little penknife!"

59

Incredulity. An inhalation from a dozen throats, then a slow breathing out, a giant sigh.

Hand in a pocket of her jeans, Torrey convulsively clutched a chocolate bar so tightly that she could feel the knobby lumps that were almonds. She looked over at Inspector O'Hare. He was leaning back against his desk, feet crossed; he was caressing his chin and soberly regarding Ms. Brenda Plant. A trill of whispers rippled among the listeners, then died; they waited.

"You tricked me," Brenda Plant said softly to Inspector O'Hare. "*You knew*. You and Ms. Tunet. Because you found out that Natalie Cameron wasn't the only one who'd maybe killed Rafe. You found out that it could've been that Kate Burnside bitch over there who'd killed him. Or me. You found out because of Ms. Tunet, her snooping, lying, stealing. Wasn't that it?"

Inspector O'Hare nodded; appalling as it seemed, his lips twitched, but he resisted looking over at Ms. Torrey Tunet, snoop, liar, thief.

"But you didn't know which of us, Inspector, did you? You and Ms. Tunet."

"Quite right, Ms. Plant."

"Of course. I see. You already have my fingerprints on the penknife, haven't you, Inspector?"

"Yes, Ms. Plant." It was in the sheaf of papers on his desk. "Forensics checked them against your fingerprints that were taken from a photograph of the cottage that Ms. Tunet rents from Castle Moore." Inspector O'Hare hesitated; he had an absurd feeling that he should apologize to Ms. Brenda Plant, murderess. But tricking her had been the only way. He'd pushed stubbornly on until with that one involuntary *No!* Ms. Brenda Plant had given herself away. Crafty, this *informal.* Not exactly Hamlet, with his play within a play to work upon Claudius, murderer of his father. Still, it had served.

Over on his left, Kate Burnside gave a kind of sobbing laugh of relief and hugged her shoulders.

As for Natalie Cameron, a still figure on the folding chair between Dakin and Sean O'Boyle, her hazel eyes were regarding Brenda Plant with fascination.

"It was an accident," Brenda Plant said, and once again it was as though she and Inspector O'Hare were quite alone in comfortable chairs, drawn up before a fireplace with a crackling fire. "I followed Rafe from Nolan's. My ankle hurt, it was agony. I didn't even know if he was going to meet his 'cuddly' or if he was going to the cairn for the blackmail money. I didn't know!" She shook her head and one of the curved combs holding her hair back slid down so that a fluff of hair fell across her brow.

"He reached the cairn. And waited. So did I, back among the trees. Then I saw Natalie Cameron arrive to meet him. Watching, I could see she'd brought no money. She was frantic but helpless, a frightened little animal. She ran off, stumbling and crying."

Brenda Plant stopped for a moment, staring back at that Tuesday noon.

"When she was gone, I limped up. I accused Rafe of

betraying me with some loose village woman. He laughed and put the penknife he was holding down on the cairn and lit a cigarette. But when I went on about what I'd heard, that he was seen going into a barn with his 'cuddly,' he got furious and struck me *here*." She lifted her chin and pulled down the front her high-necked lavender sweater; the bruise on her neck still showed red and purple and yellow. "On my throat! It could have killed me!" She settled the neck of her sweater back up and smoothed a hand down the lapel of her navy jacket. "He'd forgot that I'm the Warrior Maiden! Most of the violence in the movies was fake. But the parts I did with stones and knives were real. The way I looked at Rafe then, I could see him remembering and he dropped the cigarette and grabbed up the penknife. But I got hold of his wrist and . . . and then—It was an accident!" Brenda Plant raised a trembling hand and reset the curved comb in her hair. "An accident!"

In the silence that followed, Kate Burnside took a flat silver flask from her purse, unscrewed the cap, and raised the flask and drank. Sergeant Bryson, stiff-faced, studied his fingernails. Winifred Moore, chewing on an empty cigarette holder with her strong teeth, muttered something around it to Sheila Flaxton, meanwhile grinning over at Torrey Tunet.

Inspector O'Hare took a deeply satisfying breath. He was thinking with anticipatory pleasure of his forthcoming report to Chief Superintendent Emmet O'Reilley at Dublin Castle. Then he'd call Gilly, in forensics.

He looked over at Natalie Cameron. Vindicated. The gavel in a Dublin court would not, after all, descend and crush her.

But . . . Inspector O'Hare moved his shoulders uncomfortably inside his blue jacket. That other. Her secret now exposed. Dakin's patrimony.

"Oh, Ms. Tunet! I'm so excited! I had a part in it, didn't I! The blue jay!" Marcy McGann of the orangy red hair, the pretty face, and the gargantuan appetite was at Torrey's side. Torrey saw that Marcy was the only one who'd gotten up, the others all still sat, waiting for . . . for *what*? Did they expect to see Inspector O'Hare put chains on Ms. Brenda Plant, who still walked with a cane?

"It's so ex*citing*!" Marcy said, "Maybe I'll be interviewed on RTV. And in the papers! Mightn't I be, Ms. Tunet?"

"You might be, Marcy."

"Ahh . . . that other, Ms. Tunet. About . . ." Marcy hesitated, blushed. "You know. About Dakin Cameron. His father being . . . someone else. That's too bad."

"Yes, Marcy." Too bad. No unalloyed joy for Natalie Cameron, alas. Nor for Dakin. Photographers would be snapping pictures of the sixteen-year-old inheritor of Sylvester Hall, the boy whose father was the Sylvesters' ex-chauffeur. It would be on the RTV eight o'clock *Guess What?* program to which everyone in Ireland seemed currently addicted. The smarmy gossip sheets would be gleeful and full of guesses: Surely Marshall West, a man of the highest integrity, would break off his engagement to Natalie Cameron! Or not? In pubs across Ireland, folks would place bets.

"Bye," Marcy said, and went off.

A clank and rattle from the soda machine. Willie Hern. The village clock struck two. Torrey sighed; she had a sudden desperate need for Jasper. Damn it! Why wasn't he here instead of off at the Kinsale Food Fair stuffing himself with delicacies and gourmet dinners? Or at least—

The door of the Garda station opened.

60

Jasper. Not in Kinsale. Here. Looking rumpled and wearing that sweater with the horizontal stripes that made him look twenty pounds heavier. Torrey felt that warm, cozy, amused, loving feeling she'd had from the day she'd first met him a year ago. What in *hell* was he doing here?

"Oh, God! The press!" Kate Burnside said to nobody in particular. "That's Jasper Shaw. He must get the news by osmosis. I thought he scoped out bigger things like a New IRA bombing. Not a provincial little village murder."

Sergeant Bryson tensed and looked questioningly at Inspector O'Hare; never mind that Shaw lived half the time in that cottage with Ms. Torrey Tunet.

"I'm afraid, Mr. Shaw," O'Hare began, then stopped. Jasper Shaw had seen Ms. Torrey Tunet over there, leaning against the wall, he was already at her side and saying loud enough for O'Hare to overhear, "I have something—I wanted to get here earlier. The traffic—What do they know, so far?"

Inspector O'Hare, his blood pressure rising, said sharply, "Mr. Shaw! You are in this room on sufferance! Now, if you'll please—"

"Oh, sorry!" Mr. Shaw was unflustered. "Been following

this Ricard case closely, Inspector. Getting a bit ahead of myself. Not, believe me, Inspector, that I'd make any attempt to . . ." He grinned at O'Hare.

To scoop the Gardai, O'Hare finished grimly to himself, *to leave us with our faces red,* and Chief Inspector Emmet O'Reilley thinking Inspector Egan O'Hare in Ballynagh is a waste of Garda Síochána money. Well, too late, Mr. Shaw. He folded his arms, feeling smug.

"Mr. Shaw. I will prepare a statement for the *Irish Independent.* In essence: regarding the murder of Mr. Ricard, we have a confession from Ms. Brenda Plant of Buffalo, New York."

"Well, now!" Mr. Shaw's eyebrows rose in surprise. "Indeed!" His glance sought out Brenda Plant. She was mechanically settling and resetting the two curved combs in her hair; she seemed oblivious of anyone's presence, or even of where she was.

"So, Mr. Shaw," Inspector O'Hare continued, with satisfaction, "Ms. Natalie Cameron is absolved from suspicion. For any further information on that score, Mr. Shaw, you can refer to her attorney in Dublin." And thank God that at least Jasper Shaw wasn't accompanied by a news photographer.

Jasper Shaw sent a congratulatory smile toward Natalie Cameron. Her white-lidded hazel eyes looked back at him with faint curiosity. Dakin, beside her, seemed numb; wherever he was in his mind, it was not here in this Garda station.

Inspector O'Hare abruptly wished Jasper Shaw would disappear in a puff of smoke. He knew the reputation of this investigative reporter. A smudge of dust, a feather, an incautious word; Mr Shaw could find a clue or an answer in the shape of a snowflake.

But Mr. Shaw wasn't disappearing. He was, instead, saying, "Congratulations, Inspector. I hope I can call and set up a personal interview with you for the *Independent?* On exactly how you solved this perplexing murder."

Inspector O'Hare nodded, but for the moment he felt embarrassingly overinflated. He eyed the somewhat rumpled and overweight Mr. Shaw.

"Meantime, Inspector," Mr. Shaw said, "Just one thing: about a connection between the murder of Mr. Ricard and the attack on Mr. Brannigan, I have learned that—"

"Not again!" Dakin Cameron was on his feet, "Not to hear it *again*! That he's my father! *Brannigan!*"

"Darling!" Tears in Natalie Cameron's eyes.

"Ah," Jasper Shaw nodded. "I did hear something of the like, that's my business, ear to the ground. Found it worth investigating."

Inspector O'Hare swallowed. He pulled open his desk drawer and shook a fruit drop into his hand and popped it into his mouth. What he really wanted was a shot of whiskey. Barely three feet away, Dakin Cameron sank back down again beside his mother. He put his elbows on his knees and dropped his head in his hands.

Jasper Shaw said, "Turn over a bit of turf, that's the thing. God knows what you'll find. An old army boot. Buried treasure. A map of Atlantis. Excalibur. A hub cap." He glanced at Torrey Tunet beside him. "Ms. Tunet gave me certain information. It led me to do a bit of investigating in Dublin this morning. My investigation involved a car accident that occurred one autumn evening in Dublin, some seventeen years ago." He hiked up the side of his horizonally striped sweater and drew a slip of paper from his pants pocket:

"October twelfth. Two young women driving in a Rolls in rain and fog. The Rolls crashed into a streetlight on Heytesbury Street. Luckily the accident was not far from Meath Hospital, and the young women were taken there. One of them was uninjured. But the other young woman suffered a damaged arm and a concussion."

Jasper Shaw paused. "Or rather, at first it was *supposed*

that those two injuries were all. But the young woman had suffered a *third* injury due to the car accident. It became evident during her overnight stay at the hospital. At approximately midnight, the young woman had a miscarriage and was delivered of a female fetus."

61

Two hours later, at Sylvester Hall, Jessie was excitedly on the telephone to Rose at Castle Moore. "I didn't understand the half of it! Mr. Shaw explaining and then Ms. Burnside jumping in all of a sudden. Between them, I could hardly — It was all about a piece dropping right out of Mrs. Cameron's memory! *Months!* And not even knowing she'd lost a baby girl! So then, Dakin conceived, like on the very *heels* of — Oh, my!" and here Jessie lost her breath. Anyway, Breda was motioning to her to get the tea things ready, it was almost four o'clock.

Inspector O'Hare watched as Sergeant Jimmy Bryson began lifting stones from the cairn. The pile of stones was at least two feet high and maybe three hundred years old, from the time of Cromwell. There was moss and dirt and bits of weed and grass and pebbles on top, and even a few shards of glass. Then —

"Got it!" Bryson reached down and picked it up carefully between two fingers and handed it to O'Hare.

"Sinbad." O'Hare studied the butt. "Same as the pack among his things from Nolan's." As Brenda Plant had said, he dropped the cigarette and grabbed up the knife. Would this help in her defense? Maybe. An hour ago, two Gardai had arrived in a police car and taken her off to Dublin.

O'Hare took a breath. He looked over the fields. For a moment it was as though a frigid, wintery wind froze his marrow. What if, when the exasperating Ms. Tunet had invaded his office in her red slicker, he hadn't broken free of his exasperation at her poking her nose in where it wasn't wanted? What if? But once again, he had played her game, not quite daring *not* to.

"Wind from the north," Jimmy Bryson said, seeing him shudder. "Getting cold."

"Yes," O'Hare said. Cold as the gaze of Chief Superintendent Emmet O'Reilley would have been on him, had it later been discovered he'd gone down the wrong path. And, given Ms. Tunet being who she was, it would have been discovered. Touch and go.

On Saturday morning at ten o'clock in the library at Sylvester Hall, Dakin looked from his mother to the visitor.

It was strange, his mother smiling at the thin, pale, good-looking man who'd written the prize-winning book called *The Dakin Poems*. For a whole, agonizing night and day, Dakin had believed this Canadian to be his father. And then, not. He could tell that Tom Brannigan still loved his mother, the way he looked at her. But now his mother loved Marshall West, who'd arrived last night from New York and had put his arms around Dakin's mother and rocked her a bit saying stupid loving things like, "You should have called me!" and "I would've killed him!" Then Marshall had gone off to a low-cost housing meeting in Dublin. Now his mother, looking happy, was talking with the visitor, who looked, well, wistful, if that was a word you could use about a grown man.

"Ma?" Dakin said suddenly "What's *Cloverleaf?*"

"Cloverleaf? That's the name of the company in Bray that

mailed me my pregnancy test results." She looked at Tom Brannigan. "Mr. Ricard was holding it over my head. To return in exchange for the blackmail money."

Tom Brannigan said, in his light, cultured voice with the touch of brogue, "The Cloverleaf? I was drunk enough to've told Ricard about it, but it's in my safe deposit box in Montreal."

"*What?*" But then she laughed and put a hand up to her eyes, and the bracelet with the unicorns made a tinkling sound. She would wear the bracelet now and again. Marshall would have to cope.

"Well!" Sheila Flaxton said to Winifred, who was pulling on a plaid jumper for their before-lunch walk. There was even frost in the air and Sheila was well bundled up and had her Finnish gloves on already. "Well, Winifred. I saw Tom Brannigan in the village putting his bag into his car. He's off."

"A tragedy," Winifred said, "A damned tragedy! He's lost his son. In his head for all of sixteen years, Dakin was his son. His pride and joy. Saving reports of Dakin's tennis trophies, his wrestling matches, his school prizes."

"Yes, dreadful."

"Still . . . Maybe now he can let go of the dream of uniting with Natalie and Dakin. He's what? Barely forty? Not too late to wake up from the dream. To look about, start a new life. Even to—"

"To fall in love!" Sheila gave such an ecstatic wiggle that her woolen shawl almost slipped off her shoulders. "I am abso*lutely* with you there, Winifred!"

Noontime, Sergeant Jimmy Bryson came into Finney's for his midday meal. He was getting over his injured feelings that Inspector O'Hare hadn't briefed him beforehand about what he'd been up to at that meeting. Colluding with Ms. Torrey

Tunet! Jimmy had spent a sleepless night about it, and on top of that, the shock about Brenda. *Brenda!* In the morning, Bryson had shaved with a trembling hand and nicked the side of his chin. But at eight o'clock when he got to the station, Inspector O'Hare had hot tea going and Bryson's favorite apple-cinnamon bun and had explained, "Knowing your, ah, fondness for Ms. Brenda Plant . . ." and so on. Bryson had to admit he could see that. *Brenda!* It would be a while before he'd get over it. Still, in a way, a relief.

"Here you are." Mary, Finney's wife, set down the plate, hot corned beef, boiled potatoes and mustard pickles. Jimmy's mouth watered. And tonight was Hannah's night off; they were going to a film in Dunlavin.

"Good morning, Mr. O'Boyle."

Sean stopped raking the gravel. He hadn't heard her biking up. She was wearing that turquoise-and-gold peacocks bandana around her head and a dark red jumper and jeans. She ought to get new brogues, they were scuffed and worn.

"Morning, Ms. Tunet." *Tunet.* Lucinda had said it meant "thunder" in Romanian.

Ms. Tunet was smiling at him. "Ms. Cameron safe, after all! Been quite an ordeal for her. And of course for everyone at Sylvester Hall. You've been here the longest, Mr. O'Boyle. You've seen Natalie grow up. So I can imagine how worried *you* must've been." It was almost a question. Ms. Tunet seemed to be waiting.

"Yes," Sean said. He moved the rake a bit on the gravel.

Ms. Tunet yawned. She was still sitting on the bike, "It was electrifying at the meeting when Mr. Shaw told what he'd discovered. About what happened that night at Meath Hospital." Ms. Tunet put a forefinger to her chin. "I guess Ms. Sybil was the only one who knew about the spontaneous abortion. What with her getting the bill from Meath Hospital."

"I expect so." Under his hand, the rake handle felt slippery. It was dry weather but the sun was hot.

"At the meeting, you mentioned that in those earlier years, you were the one who picked up the morning post. Remember?"

"Yes. I suppose." He moved the rake a little on the gravel, a bit to the left there, it was humped up, it needed evening off.

"After all these years, you probably wouldn't remember any particular letter, of course. The one from Meath Hospital, I mean." Ms. Tunet heaved a sigh. "Life is peculiar, isn't it, Mr. O'Boyle?"

Sean looked up from the gravel; for an instant he looked into Ms. Tunet's gray eyes, then he turned away. "I've things to do in the greenhouse, Ms. Tunet."

"Oh, sorry!" Ms. Tunet put one foot on a bike pedal. "Stingy, wasn't she? — Ms. Sybil. So I've heard. Even saving a few cents over lamb chops! *Hon*estly!" She pushed off. Sean watched her down the avenue.

At one o'clock, Sean arrived home for the usual hour off that he allowed himself. Caitlin was out somewhere and had left a loaf and some sliced ham on the table for him. He took a piece of the ham and stood munching it. Then he went upstairs.

In his bedroom, he unlocked the top bureau drawer and took out the envelope from Meath Hospital addressed to Sybil Sylvester. He unfolded the bill. A list of charges for drugs, therapy, even surgery. What it came to was treatment of arm injury, concussion, spontaneous abortion.

Back then, when he was the one who picked up the Sylvester Hall post, he'd found the bill. It had arrived the week after Ms. Sybil had taken Natalie off to Italy in such a hurry. Sean had thought of that hurried departure as a kind of kidnapping, as though Ms. Sybil had placed a hand over

Natalie's mouth and tied her hands behind her back. He'd heard things, seen things—kitchen talk.

He'd had no excuse for opening the envelope. All he had was a kind of worry about Natalie. Then he'd opened the bill. A week after, he'd paid it. He knew Ms. Sybil wasn't one to ring up the hospital asking for a bill she hadn't received. Later, through the years, he often thought how Sybil Sylvester would always believe that Dakin was the chauffeur's son.

Now he folded the bill back into the envelope and put it into a pocket of his windbreaker. Then he knelt down and pulled open the bottom drawer. He unwrapped the tissue and shook out the yellow party dress. He could still see the ugly look on Ms. Sibyl's porcelain-stiff face as she'd thrust the yellow dress deep into the trash bin that would be emptied into Egan's cart. Why he had rescued it, he didn't know. No more did he know why he had kept it.

Downstairs, he added peat to the coal fire that Caitlin had left. Then he thrust the bill from Meath Hospital and the yellow party dress into the fire and watched them burn. After that, he made tea to go with the bread and ham. Sitting at the table and eating, he thought of when he'd first known about the thing gone wrong in Natalie's head, that had now gone right again. It was about the dog. When she'd got back from Meath Hospital, she'd come out to the greenhouse where he'd been working, she'd come to ask after a newborn pup a week old. "Tom," she'd said, "is he coming along all right?" But the pups were five months old and there was no Tom.

A week later, Dakin drove the Jeep down the rutted road and stopped beside the O'Sullivan's barn. There was a brisk wind, so that tree branches creaked and dry leaves skittered across the road. Dakin sat for a minute in the car, hands resting on the steering wheel. The blue BMW with its mud-splashed sides was gone; it wouldn't be seen here again. The barn already looked neglected—one of the windowpanes above the door was broken. Why he had come, he couldn't have said. But this time he came without his usual desperate need, drawn back helplessly to this barn, thirsting for the feel of her hands and the soft, chuckling laugh, and the need at first as though he were an inexperienced girl surrendering, and then he became a boy, and then a man, yet each time he was more and more in thrall, bewitched, no will of his own. Kate. Kate.

She was gone now, even her Georgian house in Dublin shut up. Majorca for the winter. Then, who knew where. She got about, mostly in Europe.

Dakin backed up and turned the Jeep around. It hadn't rained for a week; driving off, he could still see the tracks made by that dirty, mud-splashed blue BMW. "Why clean it?" Kate had once said, screwing up her face. "Everyone knows that under the muck it's a beauty."

62

A knock on the cottage door. Or was it the wind rattling a branch against a windowpane? It was late afternoon, a cold, brisk wind curling around the cottage, but in the kitchen there was the warmth from the fire.

Alone in the cottage, Torrey had just finished packing her carry-on and brought it into the kitchen. She'd packed the essentials first: jump rope. A Georges Simenon in Hungarian. The peacock bandanna. A peanut butter sandwich and a couple of chocolate bars for the flight, because who knew? Then the rest, including dangling black jet earrings and the fake diamond necklace and sleeveless black dress in case of a diplomatic dinner, and jeans and sneakers in which to roam Budapest.

She put the carry-on beside the kitchen dresser. She would travel in her warm but lightweight parka, under it her tailored suit and white shirt, on her wrist the man-sized Timex with date, day, and world-time sweep hands, too big for her narrow wrist, but vital to her business. At six o'clock tomorrow morning, Jasper would drive her to the Dublin airport. Then he'd continue north to Cavin, some sort of political agitation.

There, again! Definitely, someone knocking, though light, light. She crossed to the door and opened it.

"Well, hello!" In pleased surprise, she looked down at her small visitor. "Your hair! How lovely!"

Lucinda no longer wore the billed cap, her head lice must be gone. With her burnished-looking curly brown hair, she was pretty to see. Sweet little chin and sea green eyes looking innocent as sea shells.

"Come in, Lucinda. I'm glad to see you."

Standing in the kitchen, Lucinda didn't even take off her mittens. "I have my piano lesson. I only came by because Dakin said that . . . that if it weren't for you. You know. So, thank you."

"Thank *you*, Lucinda. If it hadn't been for you . . ."

"Well, good-bye."

Windy and cold as it was, Torrey watched from the open doorway as Lucinda skirted the pond and went through the hedge. Then she closed the door and went and stood close to the fire. She smiled. She was hearing Jasper say, as they lay in bed a week ago, his arm under her head, "My compliments. You played it fast and loose. But what if Kate Burnside hadn't spoken up that she'd been making love in the meadow with Brenda Plant's lover? Admittedly, you brought that horse to water. But it was pure luck that it drank."

At that, drowsily, she'd said, "Luck? Oh, no! If Kate Burnside hadn't spoken up, I'd have had to drag in Lucinda to tell that she'd seen them making love. I hated the thought of using Lucinda. Though maybe she would've liked it. I never can tell with kids." She'd nestled closer to Jasper, he was so warm and solid.

"So . . . You and O'Hare. Between you, with a nudge here and a shove there, you forced Brenda Plant into a corner."

"It wasn't easy. About on a par with the Hungarian subjunctive."

Jasper had suddenly hugged her close. "Kudos to you, my pretty."

Kudos. From the Greek *kydos*. Praise. But it had been scary. All though the meeting her heart had been thumping: Because she hadn't actually known. The frightening part was that it *could* have been Kate Burnside who'd killed the blackmailer. The only way to know that it hadn't been Kate had been to play it out, she and her enemy, Inspector O'Hare. It had been agonizing.

"How did you—?" she began, then stopped. Jasper wouldn't tell her; he never did. How he had gotten access to what musty hospital files she was never to know.

Now, after Lucinda's visit, she stood gazing into the fire. Risky, heart stopping. But it had worked out. What *norac!* *Norac.* Luck. One of her Romanian father's words, he had believed in luck, had left North Hawk in search of it.

But of course, with her, it wasn't *norac.* Always she'd made her own luck. Only she called it persistence. Jasper called it her stubbornness.

She stretched and took a deep, satisfied breath, then looked at the clock. Jasper would be coming back from the village with the lamb chops and zucchini, he'd gone on foot, wanting the exercise, saying he'd begun to look like something in a fun-house mirror.

She put on a heavy sweater and went outside. The wind had lessened, there was a moon, it made the dark woods silvery, and cast a gleam on the pond. She thought of the family at Sylvester Hall and she thought of the Dublin-to-Cork bus driver and his *Get off my bus with yor fookin' drugs!* to the two skinny Dublin boys with pipe stem legs, and how lucky for her that Dakin had appeared . . . Dakin who later came to make her a window frame.

Then she went past the pond and through the hedge onto the road to meet Jasper.